NO ONE
IN
THE GARDEN
OF
SYN

D0372789

BOOK ONE IN **THE GARDEN OF SYN** TRILOGY

MICHAEL SEIDELMAN

**Chewed
Pencil
Press**©

Copyright © 2016 Michael Seidelman

All rights reserved. No part of this publication may be reproduced, distributed, or transmitted in any form or by any means, including photocopying, recording, or other electronic or mechanical methods, without the prior written permission of the publisher, except in the case of brief quotations embodied in critical reviews and certain other noncommercial uses permitted by copyright law.

This is a work of fiction. Names, characters, businesses, places, events and incidents are either the products of the author's imagination or used in a fictitious manner. Any resemblance to actual persons, living or dead, or actual events is purely coincidental.

Printed in the United States of America. Seidelman, Michael. No One Dies in the Garden of Syn / Michael Seidelman p. cm. ISBN 978-0-9949695-0-7. Young Adult—Fiction. 2. Fantasy —fiction. 3. Cystic fibrosis — medical 4. Teen romance —fiction 5. Alternate Worlds — fiction. First Edition

Cover Design by KimG-Design.com, Copyright © 2016 Chewed Pencil Press

ISBN 978-0-9949695-0-7 (tr. pbk)

Dedicated with love to Mom & Dad

Prologue

Gone in a Flash

NOT A DAY GOES BY that Synthia Wade does not recall the night her parents disappeared. However, the night that changed her life forever began no differently than any other.

Five-year-old Synthia took a bath, put on pajamas, brushed her teeth, and swallowed some pills. Her father came into her bedroom at 7:30. He turned on the humidifier, tucked her in, and kissed her on the forehead.

"I love you," he said with a smile.

She smiled back. "I love you too, Daddy."

Her mother sat down next to her and read her favorite story, *The Gingerbread Man*. Although Synthia did not yet know how to read, she recited the last line of the story in unison with her mom. "You can't catch me, I'm the Gingerbread Man!" She giggled.

Her mom grinned as she closed the book and then handed her daughter the blue inhaler. Synthia puffed twice and handed it back, then puffed on the orange inhaler. Her mom patted her back until the coughing subsided.

After pulling the cord on the unicorn lamp, Synthia's mom bent down to kiss her forehead. "Good night, Sweetie. I love you."

"I love you too," Synthia replied, not realizing this was the last time she would reciprocate her mother's love.

Her mother left the door slightly ajar. Synthia took a tissue from the night table, wiped her nose, and held the tissue in her hand expectantly. She rolled over and rested her head on her arm. There were a few more sniffles and in a couple of minutes, Synthia was sound asleep.

* * *

"Honey," Synthia heard her mom say, "You need to wake up."

"Is it morning?" she asked, yawning and squinting on account of the bright ceiling light.

"No, Sweetie. Not yet."

Synthia's nose was dripping. Her mom wiped it and her upper lip with a tissue. "Your dad and I are going to take you somewhere. Some place wonderful. But we have to leave really soon so you need to get out of bed right away."

"Can't we wait until morning?"

"I'm afraid not, Sweetie. We have to get you dressed and leave tonight. You will love where we are going. I promise."

Synthia reluctantly sat up and allowed her pajama top to be pulled off. The bottom of the undershirt had just been lifted when Synthia's father walked in.

"Deb, Masie is outside."

Her mother's face turned white. She pressed her palms against each side of Synthia's face. "Sweetie, we'll be back in a few minutes. Please get dressed."

After they left the room, Synthia listened to them thumping down the stairs, opening the front door and slamming it shut.

She was tired, not to mention bewildered, and didn't want to go anywhere. She lay down, coughed lightly, and fell back asleep in less than a minute, despite the gleaming ceiling light above. If she had stayed awake for just one minute longer, she would have heard yelling outside, and seen a bright white light flashing through the window.

When Synthia woke, there was enough sun shining in, even with the blinds shut, that she didn't notice the ceiling light was still on. She rubbed her eyes, wiped her runny nose with a tissue, and coughed until her throat was clear. She took a sip of water from the cup on her night table and checked the time; 9:32 A.M. She was late for kindergarten. Her mom usually awakened her at 7:30. Was that a dream, when her mom shook her awake last night? If not, why didn't she come back?

Synthia coughed a few more times, put on some slippers and left the room. Her parents' bedroom was empty. So were all the bathrooms and the bedrooms. The living room was empty, as were the dining room and kitchen. She tried to turn the knob on the basement door, but it was locked as always. She looked through the kitchen window into the gardens out back and didn't see so much as a bird.

Synthia was more confused than worried. In the kitchen, she took her morning pills with a vanilla shake. The back door was slightly ajar, so she pulled the doorknob and stepped outside, curious.

A light wind ruffled her undershirt and pajama bottoms. A robin landed on a tree in the garden as a breeze rustled its leaves. There was no sign of her parents. Holding the handrail, she descended the stairs and peeked inside the carport. Both her parents' cars were parked there. Now Synthia was no longer just confused. She was worried.

The basement window on the right side of the carport had always been covered by blinds, so she couldn't see in. She knocked on the glass, hoping her parents were down there as they often were. Quiet taps at first, then harder and louder. Nothing. A tear rolled down her cheek, followed by another.

Now Synthia was more than worried; she was scared. She left the carport and went to the front of the house. The mailman was walking up the driveway.

Concerned to see this little girl, partially clothed and crying in the driveway, he bent down to her level. "Are you okay? Where are your parents?"

Synthia broke down, tears flooding from her eyes. Through the phlegm building up in her throat, she managed a quiet, yet desperate reply. "I don't know."

Chapter 1

Syn

MOST GIRLS I KNOW WOULD describe today as the worst day of their life. Not me. Most girls I know would say they just want to die after experiencing what I went through today. *Definitely* not me. What I want is to bury my head in a pillow and make the world around me disappear. Just for a little while.

If I wore mascara, my face would resemble a raccoon's. I wipe tears away with the back of my hand and angrily compose myself before exiting the school. As I sulk down the hallway, kids stare as they always do—with disdain or pity; sometimes it's hard to know which. I shove open the exit doors, banging them against the wall, and am striding toward the ramp when I hear the doors open again.

"Syn!"

Syn. Short for Synthia. I don't know why my parents spelled my name with an "S" but if I could ask them anything that would be my last question. Aunt Ruth tells me it's likely because I was special and deserving of a unique spelling. I highly doubt that's it.

Ebby Davis is out of breath but manages to catch up with me, despite her hefty build slowing her down. Her hand reaches for my shoulder. I make a sudden turn and scamper down the concrete stairs instead of the ramp.

"Syn, wait! I saw what happened."

"Leave me alone, Ebby," I say without turning around.

Ebby trundles down the steps. "You need a friend."

I still don't look back, and put more distance between us. "I need to be alone."

Cold, yes. But it worked. The sound of her footsteps fades as I turn down the sidewalk in front of the school. Certain I've lost her, I stop and cough for a full minute, expelling all the phlegm that has been building in my chest.

Most people would say that Ebby Davis is my best friend. They'd be wrong. Yes, I spend more time with her than anyone else at school, but we're in each other's lives because no one else will be.

We've been "friends" since the second month of eighth grade. We were sitting in French class when the teacher was called to the office. Katelyn, a cheerleader and one of the most popular girls in school, was sitting behind Ebby. Repeatedly, Katelyn poked a pencil through Ebby's short, curly hair. When Ebby turned around and asked her to stop, Katelyn responded by jabbing the pencil into Ebby's forehead.

"I'd rather not. You have a problem with that, Blubberbutt?"

Almost the entire class burst into laughter. That's what kids are like.

When Ebby turned around, Katelyn picked up a workbook and whacked it against the back of Ebby's head. And then again. And again. Tears rolled down Ebby's cheeks as Katelyn, almost leisurely, kept hitting her with the book, while reciting a litany of insults about her weight.

That wasn't my problem. My problems make Ebby's seem like a Sunday at the beach. Her eyes gave her away though; she didn't have the strength to stand up for herself. I felt pity for her, and didn't like the way that made me feel.

I quickly stood up. Too quickly. Mucus rushed into my throat and I started to cough, sounding like a chain smoker. The laughter quieted and the class's attention turned to me. The coughing spell continued for what seemed like forever. After it subsided, I stared at Katelyn and simply said, "Leave her alone." Then I carefully sat back down.

The class remained silent. While staring at my desk, I could feel Ebby's eyes on me, in appreciation and probably, admiration. Not that I deserved either one.

Now we are in tenth grade and she's glued to my side. I don't mind. It beats being alone a lot of the time. But I don't have the affection for her that you're supposed to have for a *real* friend. There is a difference. Ebby surely feels the same way, though sometimes I wonder if she doesn't realize it, not having any other friendships to compare it to.

The walk home from school takes about twenty minutes. For the first eight minutes, the route leads through subdivisions with reasonably sized houses that are about thirty years old, then veers into the Southlands area. Large and small houses sit on ten- to twenty-acre properties. Most of them back onto farmland of some sort—livestock, horse stables, blueberry farms, cornfields, and vegetables. Many who live in Redfern, Washington, have never ventured out here and some don't even know the area exists.

While turning the corner onto my street, the sense that someone is following me takes hold. I spin around but there's no one in sight. The feeling of being watched or followed occurs frequently but there's never anyone there. I'm probably just paranoid.

My house is on one of the few properties in the area that doesn't have any type of farmland or barns. It was a hundred and fifty years ago when my mother's great-grandfather built it. By the time my mom inherited it, the farm had been converted into a fabulous botanical garden.

After walking down the long driveway, I study the modest, white Tudor-style house in front of me. More than a hundred and fifty years old, the two-story house looms over me as if it were a living entity.

I climb the stairs to the front door and enter the house, shutting the door behind me and tossing my jacket into the corner of the foyer. My aunt is sitting at the kitchen table. Our cat, Fluffy (an ironic name since she's a hairless Sphynx), is sitting on the windowsill, scanning the yard for birds she'd like to kill.

Aunt Ruth dog-ears the page of the magazine she was reading and presses it closed. Small square glasses and straight blonde hair cut at her neckline give her the appearance of a librarian, which is fitting since this was her occupation before moving to Redfern to take care of me. She always has her face in a book, magazine, or newspaper, and I can't help but wonder if there is regret about letting her career go.

Aunt Ruth stands up. There is concern on her face. She couldn't possibly know about what happened at school. How could she?

"How was school, Syn?"

It's clear she's about to tell me something I don't want to hear. Then it hits me hard. Janna. "What's wrong?"

"Why don't you sit down?" My aunt puts her hand on my shoulder. I shrug it off.

I pull out a chair and sit. Not because I want to, but because my knees feel like they will buckle at any moment.

"Janna. Did she—" I choke on the lump in my throat. "Did she—"

"No, but she's not doing well. Her mom said she probably doesn't have much time left. I'm sorry, Syn."

I push my chair backward with my feet and somehow find the strength to stand up.

"I want to go see her. Now."

"It's a three-hour drive, Syn. And, too late in the day. Her mom is expecting us tomorrow morning. Janna wants to see you too."

Aunt Ruth hugs me and I don't resist.

"So sorry, Syn. I know how much she—"

I pull away. "I'm going upstairs."

"Okay. Do you want me to—"

"I just want to be alone."

I come off as frosty, but my aunt is used to it. I walk up to my room, kick my shoes off, and thump onto the bed. My head hits the pillow and I curl up on my side, staring at a picture on the night table through tear-blurred eyes. The picture of Janna and me was taken when I was seven and she was eight. If we weren't both wearing hospital gowns and I didn't have an oxygen tube in my nose, we could have been mistaken for kids at summer camp. Our smiles—because we were together—were joyful and contagious.

I met Janna a month before the picture was taken. She was in the hospital for leukemia treatments. I was there having tests done for my own ailment—cystic fibrosis.

Cystic fibrosis (CF) is a disorder that gunks up my sinuses and lungs. If my birth had been a generation ago, I would probably be dead already. Because there are much better treatments now, the average person with CF lives to about thirty-seven. Doctors have told me that my case is serious and I likely won't live past twenty.

Perhaps that's why Janna and I feel so close—neither of us expects to live to be an adult. While our similar tragic fates may have brought us together, something stronger has developed over time. We're both only children who love each other like sisters. We might not see each other every day, every week, or even every month, but I couldn't imagine a stronger friendship.

My aunt wishes our relationship was just as strong.

I had been planning to Skype Janna and tell her about my crappy day at school. My problems seem petty now, though alongside the sadness felt for my friend I'm still a little pissed off.

For the past few months, I've been dating this guy, Jon. My first boyfriend. He's not the coolest kid at school; far from it. Actually, he's quite the nerd, but that's not a bad thing in my book.

Today Jon told me he couldn't see me anymore. But that wasn't what tore me up. It was the reason. He said he was starting to care for me, and possibly falling in love. And that's why he was breaking things off. Because one day I'd die and he didn't think he could handle losing me. So he let me go, to die alone because he's too big of a wuss.

Now, instead of blowing off steam by telling my best friend—the only person I know who would totally understand—I have to bottle things up and prepare to say goodbye. *How?* It breaks my heart that a week or two from now—possibly sooner—the world will lose such a precious soul.

I turn away from the picture and press my face into the pillow. Tears soak through while phlegm is building up in my chest. Soon the coughing and gagging will start. And, if I don't calm down and take care of myself, if I cry too hard, I might even have to spend the night in the ER.

I roll onto my side and try to calm down. Tears continue to drench my pillow. I need to stop thinking about losing my best friend and prepare for the impossible—saying my final goodbye.

Chapter 2

Farewell to a Friend

FEELING HALF ASLEEP, I stumble to the fridge, pull out a carton of milk, a pitcher of orange juice, cream cheese, and eggs. I stick two slices of bread in the toaster. As the eggs are frying, I open the cupboard and reach for the remaining can from a six-pack of strawberry milkshakes. I cut each plastic ring into pieces before throwing them away; no bird or fish will get entangled or suffocate because of my laziness.

Four eggs, toast, and a milkshake might seem like a lot for a weekday breakfast. Lunch is the first meal of the day for many kids at school. But cystic fibrosis makes digesting food difficult, so I need double the calories of a healthy person my age. If my caloric intake is low, my immune system becomes vulnerable to all sorts of illnesses. Enzyme pills taken with every meal—and almost twenty additional pills every morning and night—provide me even more calories.

After breakfast, I clean up the kitchen and head to my bedroom for the physical therapy vest treatment. Twice a day, I need to put this awkward contraption on my chest, connect the tubes in it to a pump that is plugged into the wall, and sit as it vibrates. The jacket fills with air and shakes my lungs. When I'm done, it's easier to cough up the mucus that's been accumulating.

Usually I pass the time reading. This morning, I just sit on the edge of my bed thinking about Janna. Aunt Ruth comes into my room halfway through the procedure. "How are you doing?"

"I'm doing."

She likely didn't hear what I said because the pump is loud and my voice vibrates when I'm wearing the vest. It sounds like I'm talking into an electric fan. There is concern in my aunt's eyes but she attempts to console me with a smile and lets me be.

When I'm done with the vest, there are still a couple of less time-consuming procedures to complete before I can leave for the day. First, I breathe meds directly into my nose with a nebulizer. Then after cleaning the equipment (another fifteen minutes), I breathe through two puffers— one with a red sticker and one with a yellow sticker.

To stay in good physical shape and keep my immune system strong, I walk on a treadmill and do sit-ups before school. This morning, I just want to go see Janna so I skip that for now. Not too smart—could relapse later—but I tell my aunt I'm ready.

"I didn't hear you on the treadmill," my aunt says.

"I went for a walk before you woke up," I lie. If she knew I skipped part of my routine, she wouldn't let me leave until I did it.

The ride to the hospital is quiet. Aunt Ruth tries to make conversation a few times but my clipped replies shut her down quickly. She turns on the radio twice. Each time I reach out and turn it off. I stare out the window for most of the ride, ignoring the farmland that passes by behind a light wall of fog.

About two hours into the drive my aunt starts to play classical music on her phone through Bluetooth. I am about to turn it off, but the music is soothing so I decide to leave it alone. A short time later I doze off.

My aunt's hand on my shoulder nudges me awake. "We're here."

We're in a small parking lot in front of the two-story hospice. If it had a driveway instead of a parking lot, it would resemble a large house.

As we pass through two automatic glass doors, I get that familiar sense of dread, which always happens when I enter a hospital. Hospitals have helped me extensively during my short life, and yet the stench of sickness and death is impossible to ignore. The first thing we see is a spacious living room with a piano, gas fireplace, and flat-screen TV; comforting despite the unmistakable stale feeling of a hospital.

Aunt Ruth texts Janna's mom, who tells us to come up to the second floor. Janna's mom is waiting for us when we step off the elevator. She smiles but her eyes reveal pain.

Janna's mom hugs me, puts her arm around my shoulder, and leads me down the hallway to Janna's room. My aunt lingers in the hallway. I know she wants to be there for me but realizes that I'd rather she wasn't.

Janna's room is nicely decorated with scenic paintings, a couch, and a few overstuffed chairs. It still resembles a hospital room, but these nice touches give the room a warmer feeling. I'm surprised to see that Janna shares the space with two patients. You would think that when you're this close to the end they would let you have a private room. Being a hospice, I know her "roommates" are also at the final stages of their lives.

The man could be well over a hundred. He lies motionless and stares at me - eyes wide open. He doesn't blink. I wonder if he's even able to move a finger or toe. The woman in the bed next to him probably isn't any older than forty. Light shines off her smooth, bald head, which is as pale as her face. She smiles at me and I try to reciprocate. However,

I can't help but feel fury that this woman with a similar illness to Janna's has managed to hang in there so much longer than my friend. Deep in my heart though, I'm sad for her.

At the opposite end of the room, by the window, is Janna. I choke up at the sight of her. She is weak. There are bruises on her face and arms and she's wearing a horrible blonde wig. Our eyes meet and like always, we connect without saying a word.

I give her a gentle hug and want to tell her I love her, but can't get the words out. It doesn't matter though. Janna knows. She returns the affection with a tender stroke on my cheek.

Janna's mom leaves the room to give us some time alone. Tears flow down my face, yet Janna remains expressionless.

"How are you doing?" she whispers.

"Me?" I respond, surprised. "How are *you*?" I immediately regret the stupid question but know what the answer will be—one I won't ever understand.

"I'm good," she says and then repeats herself. "I'm good."

My friend isn't just putting on a show of strength. Janna has always embraced her ailment as something that was meant to be. She accepted her fate long ago. But how can she be this content when she's so close to the end?

"I know you are," I say. "You're always good."

We look into each other's eyes for a few seconds and then embrace again. After what seems like forever, I let go. The cheap wig is sitting sideways on her head. When I clutch it with my fingers, Janna's hand covers mine. For the first time since I came into the room, I see pain in her eyes.

"I don't want you to..." Janna pauses, "to see me like that. To remember me like—"

"Are you kidding me?" I interrupt, tears raining down my cheeks. "You will always be beautiful to me. No one I have ever met is as beautiful a person as you. We've seen each other at our worst. I've seen you right after chemo and surgery and you've seen me at low points that no one but you or my aunt have any idea about. You could have burn marks and scars all over your face and I'd still never be able to see you as anyone but the most beautiful person I've ever known."

A tear wells up and rolls down Janna's cheek as she pulls off the wig.

I quickly glance at her head before returning my eyes to hers. And then I say what I wanted to say before. "I love you."

"I love you too."

We hug for another long moment and then I meet her eyes again. "Be honest with me. "Are you really okay? Are you really good?"

"I really am," she says, with no need to think about her answer. "I accepted that my life was going to be short a long time ago. I had a good run. A terrific mom and the best friend—the best *sister*—any girl could ask for. How could I *not* be good?"

I wanted to be perfect like her.

She pats my head. "Are you going to be okay?"

"I don't know. When my time comes, I won't have you—"

"You'll always have me in your—"

"Of course. But you know…"

"I know." She smiles. "You're beautiful too. Never forget that."

"I don't know how you do it. How you accept things. When it's my time, I'll be wishing for a magical cure like an inmate on death row prays for the governor's pardon. To give me even a few more days."

"Do you want to know my secret?"

I already know her secret. Regardless, I nod.

"Live every day to its fullest. Enjoy every moment you have. And then when the time comes, you will have had a better life than most people who live to be ninety."

I'm not strong enough to have that positive an outlook on such a short life, but I smile and rest my head gently on her chest. She lightly strokes my hair and without a single word, our bond grows even closer than if we were siblings. We know this could be the last time we'll see each other, yet try not to think about that and just enjoy each other's company. We'll live this day to the fullest, as Janna would say.

Eventually a doctor enters the room, followed by Janna's mom and my aunt. I don't want to go but understand she needs to rest. We hug for another minute, until my aunt puts her hand on my shoulder. I kiss Janna's forehead.

Amazingly, I have more tears left in me and boy do they pour. "Love you," I tell her, choking up.

She blows me a kiss. "See you soon."

She's really saying that she hopes she'll make it through the night and that we'll visit again tomorrow. Yet I can't also help but think it means we'll meet in the afterlife shortly. She may be ready to accept this. I'm not.

As I'm walking out of the room, my lungs clogged up from my crying spell, I turn around to see the doctor pull the curtain shut and cut off Janna's smile from view. Our visit had felt perfect until that curtain separated us with such brutal finality.

My aunt doesn't turn on any music during the ride home. I stare out the window, not even thinking or daydreaming. I don't think I've ever felt emptier.

When we get home, I have a bite to eat and notice there are texts from Ebby and Jon. I had my phone set on silent and hadn't even thought to check. I didn't want to. And I don't want to now. I turn the phone off and place it on the kitchen table.

My aunt suggests I call Ebby and ask her to get any missed homework assignments from my teachers. I don't answer. I walk to the back door and look out over the deck to the only place where I can get my head in a better space. I head down the stairs toward my sanctuary, my oasis…my garden.

Chapter 3

The Garden

LOTS OF KIDS AT SCHOOL have big families and live in small, cramped apartments. They share rooms with siblings and often don't have a balcony to breathe in fresh air without leaving their building. Although the world seems to conspire against me in so many ways, I'm fortunate to live in a spacious home, and to have the most beautiful green refuge imaginable.

I walk down the concrete footpath and take in the wonders before me. While our property extends for more than six acres, from here the garden seems infinite. My parents inherited the house from my mom's parents, who were successful botanists. My late grandparents named a few of the flowers in the garden, which are now planted all around the world.

To me, the garden is a place of solace. The only place where I can simply let the breeze flow through my hair and allow my mind to go free. Sure, I still think about what ails me here too but when finished, I'm able to let it all go and it's like being in a magical world I have all to myself. In spite of me not believing in an afterlife, this garden has to be the closest thing to heaven one could experience while the heart still beats. Aside from the gardeners hired to maintain it, my aunt and I have this haven all to ourselves.

After the tall hedge, the path goes two ways. I habitually turn right. The path forms a circle so either way I arrive at the same place. Leaves rustle in the gentle breeze as my long hair flutters against my back. I twirl a strand between my fingers and admire its rich, lustrous chestnut color. A rabbit pops out of a bush and watches me with its glassy black eyes. Though there are none in sight, I can hear birds singing.

I arrive at my destination—a large, circular pond. I walk farther and step off the end of the pathway onto the lawn. A tall ornamental cherry tree stands about twenty paces from the back of the pond. The tree is in full bloom with beautiful pink flowers. I touch the trunk and find what I'm looking for. It's hard to see, but with the tips of my fingers I can easily identify a carving that was engraved over twenty years ago. DL + IW. Debra Lowery + Ian Wade. My parents' initials, carved into the tree by my father, permanently affirming his blossoming love for the woman who would eventually become his wife.

I didn't know my parents for very long. They were scientists who taught at the local university. They disappeared, along with their colleague, Masie Winters, when I was five. Not long after, three bodies were found, "burned beyond recognition," as the police told my aunt. Dental records were matched to Masie's body. The teeth from the other two bodies were too burned to attempt a match. The police assumed they belonged to my parents. Their disappearance and murders have never been solved.

I don't cry for two reasons. One reason is to prevent my symptoms from acting up. Crying builds up mucus, which leads to coughing and sore lungs. There is enough of that already without needlessly bringing on more. The other reason is that I don't believe my parents are dead. The police can think whatever they want. I believe— know—that my parents are still alive. They are out there somewhere. I'm not certain why they would leave me but they must have had their reasons. Hopefully, I will be able to see them at least one more time in my short life.

I touch the carved initials once more and then walk back to the pond. I sit down cross-legged next to the water and inhale deeply. So many wonderful scents in the air. The only sounds are the voices of nature and the faint thrum of a lawnmower in the distance. I close my eyes, lie back with my head on the lawn and fade into the majestic scenery.

Not a minute after shutting my eyes my cell phone vibrates in my pocket. I ignore it. A minute later it vibrates again. My aunt is inside and Janna doesn't have a phone, so it's got to be Ebby or Jon. I don't want to talk to either of them right now. Especially Jon.

Jon is a family friend of Ebby's. I wouldn't consider them actual friends but they talk sometimes and he always says hi to her in the hallway. Like Ebby and myself, he isn't the most popular kid at school.

Jon is taller than me, lanky and practically blind without his thick, black-rimmed glasses. No masking tape holding them together though. I'd be lying if I said he was the best-looking guy in school but he looks all right in my opinion. He was really sweet to me, and we got along well. No one had ever shown any interest in me so when he asked if I wanted to hang out I was touched—and possibly a little smitten. The moment he asked me out, this awkward, nerdy guy almost seemed—dare I say it?—kinda cute.

We dated for about three months. It was pretty PG as far as relationships go. We sometimes held hands and even kissed on a few occasions. Since he also knew Ebby, the three of us would hang out together. It all seemed good. Until about three weeks ago, when I got a lung infection and had to spend a couple of weeks in the hospital. Hospital stays are a normal part of my life. Some years I've spent up to three months in the hospital if you add up all my episodes. It sucks. The procedures are horrible, the rest of the time is boring, and you don't get out of doing your homework.

Jon knew about my CF but this was the first time since we started going out that I had stayed overnight at the hospital. He came to visit on my second day. I tried to be upbeat. Obviously, seeing me hooked up to an oxygen tank with an IV in my arm freaked him out. He wasn't himself and our conversation was awkward. He didn't stay long and only communicated by text until my release. After that he avoided me until I finally confronted him yesterday.

I snuck out of science class a few minutes early and waited outside his math class. He froze when he saw me and said he had to go to his next class, which I called bullshit on because it was the end of the day. Jon ended up breaking down and sobbing in the hall. He said he was really starting to like me and didn't think he could take losing me one day if we got any closer. I wasn't heartbroken—just pissed. My illness is something I have to deal with every minute of every day and he didn't think *he* could deal with it? I shoved him against a locker, called him something pretty nasty, and left. Ebby must have seen what had happened and followed me outside. My chest was hurting and mucus was filling my throat. I just wanted to get out of there. To be alone. And then I get home to find out my best friend—my only real friend—is… I can't even say the words to myself. She deserves to live a long and happy life. And selfishly, I need her.

Aunt Ruth loves me and I love her but it's not the same. Our relationship is somewhat odd. She gave up everything for me, even though she had only met me twice before my parents disappeared - once when I was born and once when I was three. My aunt sent me a birthday card every year but lived on the other side of the country and didn't really know me. However, when I had no one to take care of me and was living in a foster home, she quit her job as a librarian and moved home to the house she grew up in, even though she's a city person and doesn't like it. She dedicated her life to taking care of a girl she hardly knew. And not just a normal girl. A sick girl who spends lots of time in the hospital. A girl who's going to die before she does. Aunt Ruth has supported me through my worst, given me everything in her heart, and even became the head fundraiser for our local chapter of the Cystic Fibrosis Foundation.

"No one is going to find a cure sitting on their asses," she says, even though I realize there is not much chance of that happening in my lifetime. I'm thankful she's there for me, and yet also resentful because she's not my mother. That's wrong of me—horrible—yet I can't help it. It's hard to not let those feelings show but sometimes they do.

My phone vibrates again. I sigh, sit up, and pull it out of my pocket. Eight text messages. I didn't even feel that many buzzes. They go back through the day. Six from Ebby. *Hey, where r u? R u ok? Please let me know ur ok. If ur in the hospital, I will come see u. Xo xo.* And then three more of the same.

There are also two texts from Jon. *I'm so sorry to have hurt you. Can we talk?* I don't want to talk to him. He's being a little coward. At least he's mature enough to use full sentences and correct spelling when he texts though. Not to mention, his texts are always free of those horrible emojis.

I will text him soon. He can sweat a little. First, I must let Ebby know that I'm okay. I'm about to put the phone to my ear when the back of my neck suddenly feels cold and a shadow falls over me. I don't have time to turn around before a hand pushes against the top of my back. I drop the phone and fall headfirst into the pond.

Chapter 4

Drowning

As the cold surface of the water strikes my face, my mind is scrambled with confusion, dread, and fear. Water floods through my nose and mouth and into my lungs. I flay my arms and legs yet can't get my head above water.

I instinctively cough, which brings more water into my lungs. That's an absolute disaster for someone with CF. Panic sets in. Unable to turn around, and sinking deeper, far deeper than I would have believed. This pond had always seemed shallow.

My limited sight worsens. Unless someone pulls me out, I'm going to die. My life expectancy was already short but I never thought I'd go this young. I can feel my consciousness—my life—fading away. I'll never see Janna again. Or Aunt Ruth. Though it might have been naïve to have believed otherwise, I'll never see my parents again either. Or even find out what happened to them. The end is near. No, far worse. The end is *here*!

I see only black as my life begins to seep from my body. Nothing but black. And...and...the outline of something. A light. A glow. And then...

I feel groggy. As my eyes open, I'm blinded by light. No longer underwater, my breathing is normal. My first thought is that I was wrong. That there *is* an afterlife and I'm about to discover it. Then I feel a blanket over me. My body has dried but my hair is still wet. Someone must have saved me. The person who pushed me in? Perhaps it was an accident. Or maybe my aunt saw me fall in. I'm probably lying in my own bed. Safe. Safe and alive, to live another day. And hopefully a few more years after that.

I rub my eyes and my vision starts to clear. The color and layout of the room I'm in doesn't match any room in my house. There's someone sitting next to me. A young boy in a chair. Six years old, seven tops.

Then I realize that under the tucked-in blanket, I'm not wearing anything. Someone undressed me. I carefully pull my arms over the top of the blanket and hold it against my chest. I'm about to scream when the boy pushes back the chair. He stands up and runs through the open door.

"She's awake! She's awake!" he yells.

I see the top of his head swish by a window a few inches to the right of the door. My first instinct is to stand up but since I'm not wearing anything, I look around the room instead.

I'm inside a log cabin. There's a long couch in the middle of the room, facing away from the foot of my bed. A wooden kitchen table and four chairs sit beneath a large window. On either side of the window are shelves decorated with pottery and knickknacks, and portraits are hanging on the wall. Most of the pictures have a little boy in them. Perhaps the one who was just here? A middle-aged man and a woman appear in several other pictures.

A second door leads to another room. If I were on a vacation with my aunt, this would be a cozy place to stay. But how did I get here? Who undressed me and why? Probably to keep me from running away. One thing is for sure…I need to escape.

After wrapping the blanket around my scrawny body I stand up, keeping my eyes on the door and windows. While backing away from the bed to-ward the door, I notice grass and trees outside. There's no one there.

I turn to face the other door. It leads to a walk-in closet and then to another room. Clothes are hanging on one side of the closet, which are obvi-ously for the boy. Women's clothing is hanging on the other side. The outfits are considerably larger than my size but this is no time to be picky.

I grab a white dress and peek through the doorway on the other side of the closet. It leads to another room with a bed on one side and a kitchen on the other. A few feet from the bed a door opens to a bathroom. I back into the closet, drop the blanket and pull the dress over my head. Someone considerably older and heavier might wear a sundress like this. It's better than the blanket though.

After returning to the first room, I notice something. I inhale, exhale. Then, take another breath, breathing in only through my nose, and exhale. I put my hand over my chest and feel myself breathing naturally.

I must escape this place and find my aunt, but can't believe this amazing feeling. When people ask what living with cystic fibrosis is like, I tell them to imagine living with a bad cold every day of their life. Yet here I don't feel like I have any sort of cold whatsoever. I feel great!

The young boy looks at me through one of the windows and smiles. A genuine, friendly smile. I'm puzzled, although my fear has evaporated. It's uncertain where I am and why I feel so—so good, but surely I'm not being held against my will after all.

The same woman from the photo (whose dress I'm likely wearing) walks in with the boy, carrying a cloth bag. She's in her mid-forties, about an inch taller than me and has a large build.

"Well, hello."

"Hi," I nervously reply.

"You found our closet. I was just getting you some clothes that will be a better fit for you." She pulls out a plain red T-shirt and a pair of jeans. "I have undergarments for you too."

"Where am I? Were you the one who undressed me?"

"Yes. You were soaking wet when Cole found you. I dried you off and hung your clothes outside."

"Who's Cole?"

"Cole is a nice young man who lives nearby. Around your age. He found you floating in the pond."

"Why did he bring me here? My aunt was home."

The woman seems puzzled. "Who is your aunt?"

"Aunt Ruth. Ruth Lowery."

"Where does she live?"

We're both equally puzzled now. "In the house behind the pond."

I walk toward the door and the woman stands aside to let me outside into a botanical garden similar to the one behind my house. But this garden is different. In front of me are two log cabins that are narrow at the front and go back quite a way. I breathe in the lovely, natural aroma from the surrounding trees and flowers, still in disbelief at how wonderful and healthy I feel, yet as muddled as ever. Am I dead? I've always considered life after death to be a fairytale but this is all so bizarre that the afterlife is starting to sound like the most rational explanation.

I turn to the woman. "Who are you? And where am I?"

Chapter 5

The (New) Garden

"I'M ROSE," THE woman says. "This is my son, Flint."

Flint smiles. "Hi. What's your name?"

"Syn."

"Well, Syn," Rose says, "I haven't seen you around before. May I ask how you got here?"

"I don't even know where *here* is."

Rose raises her eyebrows. "Here is here."

That doesn't help one bit.

Rose smiles. "Do you remember where you were before you fell into the pond?"

"In my garden. Behind my house. In Redfern." I don't mention being pushed into the pond. Perhaps I was mistaken, and just fell in.

"Hmm." Rose's eyes narrow and she pinches her chin with her fingers.

"Do you think she came through the fog?" Flint asks, looking up at his mom.

"It's the only explanation I can think of. She couldn't have fallen from the sky."

"The fog? What fog?"

The woman sighs. "That doesn't matter. Not to me, anyhow. It's nice to have you here, Syn."

"And here is…?"

"In the Garden, of course." Rose gently places her hand on Flint's shoulder. "Honey, why don't you go find Cole? Tell him our new friend has woken up."

With a look of excitement, the boy nods and runs off.

"Are you hungry?" Rose asks.

Eating isn't something I normally look forward to. Sure, I appreciate food that tastes good but because I have a hard time digesting it, eating is more of a task than anything else. It's something I just need to do to build up calories in my system. But right now I'm actually hungry.

"I could eat something."

"Good. Let's head over to the Square and get something to eat while we wait for Cole."

As we walk across the beautifully maintained lawn behind the cabins, again I breathe in the sweet aromas flowing through the air. The scents are similar to those in my garden at home—just more vivid, because I'm no longer breathing them in through a swollen nose. For the first time in my life, I don't feel handicapped. So as perplexing as this is, I decide to just go with the flow. There doesn't seem to be much of a choice.

We pass two more cabins. Their front doors are wide open. A large, middle-aged woman leaves one cabin as we pass. A grin like I've never seen before forms on her face, emitting so much joy it's infectious.

"Well, hello!" she exclaims. "Why, if that isn't a new face."

Rose smiles at her. "It is indeed. Syn, I'd like to introduce you to Dawn."

Dawn hurries over and gives me the once-over before embracing me with her soft, brown arms. She squeezes tightly, holding me for a few seconds.

"It's so nice to meet you, Syn. It's not often we see new people around here."

I smile. A genuine smile, which isn't something people often see from me. "It's nice to meet you too." It feels as if we've met before but I can't place when or where. Maybe her positive energy has just overwhelmed me.

"We're heading to the Square to get Syn something to eat," Rose says.

"Please do stop by later," Dawn offers.

We walk around the corner and Rose says, "We're here."

The Square Rose referred to is actually a spacious, circular lawn separated from the rest of the Garden by round concrete blocks. There's a rustic wooden well at the opposite end of the Square and tables and blankets are laid out in front of the concrete blocks. Only two of the tables are occupied.

A woman around Rose's age is sitting at one table next to a girl not much older than me. The girl has straight blonde locks that seem to reflect the rays of the sun. At the table to their right sits an old man. A *really* old man. In fact, I've never seen a man so wrinkled and hard done by. Despite this, his crooked teeth gleam at me in welcome.

We go over to the first table, where fresh fruits and vegetables are displayed—apples, pears, peaches, berries, carrots, and potatoes. The old man, who's sitting at a table covered with bread and baked pastries, stands up and approaches us. One would have expected that his brittle bones would have made standing difficult, but he jumped out of his seat like a ten-year-old boy.

"Why, hello there," the old man says to me. "It's not often we see a fresh face around here. And such a lovely one at that."

He reaches out his hand and I shake it, making an effort to not squeeze too hard. He has a surprisingly strong handshake.

"Syn, this is Wolf," Rose says. She gestures to the woman and the teenage girl. "And this is Fawn and her daughter, Lily."

Fawn and Lily say hello and shake my hand, both of their handshakes gentle.

Rose tilts her head toward the table laden with food. "What would you like?"

"I don't have any money with me."

She laughs, picks up an apple, and hands it to me. "You don't need to pay. We all do our part here."

The others stare at me like they've never seen a person eat an apple before. I wipe it off with one hand and take a bite.

"Pretty good, huh?" Fawn asks.

"Yeah, it is," I agree, chewing with my mouth full. The apple is firm and sweet—quite enjoyable I find, despite never having been fond of apples. Actually, it's more than the taste that's pleasing; it's the fact that it can be swallowed without any pain or discomfort. I devour the fruit as they continue to stare.

Wolf leaps through the air like he's a high school cheerleader and then does the impossible— a backflip worthy of an Olympic medal. "She likes it!"

I stare at Wolf in awe and then at the others. No one seems perplexed. "What's wrong, Honey?" Rose asks. "Wolf just likes to show off."

"How…how did you do that?"

"How did I do what?"

"That backflip. I couldn't do that in a million years and, um, no offense, but I'm quite a bit younger than you."

"Just a bit," quips Wolf, and the others laugh.

"A man Wolf's age couldn't do that where you're from?" Lily asks.

"Of course not."

"She must have come through the fog," Wolf says.

"She says she didn't," Rose replies.

"Well, I couldn't imagine she fell from the sky," Wolf adds, repeating what Rose had said earlier.

"In our Garden, everyone is spry and healthy," Lily says. "Perfectly healthy."

"Physically, we age," Fern says. "We get wrinkles and crow's feet as time goes by. Internally, our bodies stay in perfect condition."

I can hardly believe my ears. This would explain why I feel so good. It sounds like magic. Magic isn't real though. This must be a dream.

"So no one gets sick here?"

"Sick?" Lily asks. "What's that?"

"What do people die from?"

Wolf belts out a loud laugh. "Die? That word's barely in our vocabulary. We're all in perfect health. Always and forever!"

"Forever?"

"That's right," Wolf says. "As long as we stay in the Garden and are cautious of danger, no one dies."

This is unbelievable. Still, for the first time since arriving, it's not important how I got here or how to get home. What's really important is that my health is perfect as long as I stay.

And all of a sudden, I'm in no rush to get home.

Chapter 6

The Boy with Two Faces

WITH THE STRENGTH AND EASE of a twenty-year-old man, Wolf hoists the rope from the well and delivers a large bucket of water. He uses a cup to scoop water from the bucket and hands it to me.

I gulp down the water. It's ice cold and possibly the purest I've ever tasted. Plus, being able to drink without each gulp hurting makes it taste that much better.

"More?" Wolf asks me.

I nod and guzzle down another cup.

As I head back to Rose and the others, Flint comes around the corner with another boy. A boy like no one I've seen before.

"Syn, this is Cole," Rose says. "The young man who pulled you out of the pond."

"Hello," Cole says in a deep voice. "It's nice to see you're doing well. You weren't in the best shape when I found you."

It's not easy to describe Cole. Simply put, he's a tall, well-built teenage boy, probably about seven-

42

teen or eighteen years old. However, his facial appearance seems to be made up of two different people. Sort of like the Batman villain Two-Face. Cole is anything but monstrous though. In fact, he's quite handsome. About a third of his face, on the left side, has pale complexion topped by crew-cut blonde hair. The rest of his face is considerably darker - Latino if I had to guess; the hair on that side is black. His arms and neck are colored in equal proportions to his face. Although I'm surprised by his unique appearance, I'm equally intrigued.

I offer him a handshake and he surprises me by pulling me into a hug. My heart flutters. I don't usually feel this way around boys. Not even Jon. There's just *something* about him.

"I'm so glad you're okay," he says. He loosens his muscled arms and we part.

I have to make an effort to speak coherently. "Thank you. For, you know, saving me." Not terrific, but it could have been worse.

"Of course. Things are usually pretty quiet around here and it's not every day I find a damsel in distress. Especially a damsel I've never seen before."

I'm not sure how to respond. Luckily, Rose interjects. "Syn isn't sure how she got here."

"It's nice to have you here nonetheless," he says.

"I was going to show Syn around the Garden," Rose says, "Perhaps you'd like to give her the tour."

Cole's light and dark lips form a gorgeous, eager smile. "I'd be happy to."

I ask to use the washroom and Rose leads me to her place. When I'm done, she's waiting for me outside.

"Syn, I expect you'll want to try to find your way home. Please know that you're more than welcome to stay with us for as long as you'd like. Flint likes you. He's offered to sleep on the couch and let you have his bed."

Their kindness is touching. Aunt Ruth must be worried sick by now and I really should try to find a way home. But I feel so healthy—so alive—for the first time ever. I can't leave just yet, no matter how terrible a person that makes me.

I return to the Square to meet Cole and leave worrying about getting home for later. Traipsing through the Garden, I enjoy the warmth of the sun and the light touch of wind on my skin. When I reach the Square, Wolf has left the well and Cole is splashing water from the bucket onto his face. He waves to me.

"Ready for the tour?"

"Yeah."

Cole gazes into my eyes, smiles and raises his left arm. At first it seems that he's motioning to hold my hand, until he raises his other arm and holds both hands behind his head. He stretches high, lets both arms fall, and starts walking.

"All right. Let's do this!"

There are two more cabins next to a line of trees and shrubs, with clothes flapping outside on a clothesline. Both front doors are ajar.

"Why do people leave their doors open?"

"Why wouldn't they?"

Theft and murder are two things that spring to mind; I keep those morbid thoughts to myself.

Farther back, behind the cabins, is a mysterious thick gray mist—a heavy wall of fog. It begins abruptly and is impossible to see through, unlike any fog I've ever encountered. To my left and right, it seems that the wall of fog borders the Garden. "What's this fog?"

Cole stops walking and thinks for a second. "The fog isn't someplace you want to go."

That sounds ominous. "Why not?"

"Let's just say that if there were any cabins in the fog, the owners wouldn't only keep their doors shut, they would keep them bolted up tight."

"Okay."

We walk silently for several minutes alongside the wall of fog.

Then a light bulb flashes in my head. "This must be what Rose was talking about when she asked if I got here through the fog. What's out there? Where does it take you?"

"You never know what you'll find out there."

"So no one here ever goes through it?"

"Some of us do; only when we have to. To gather supplies. The Garden has so much to offer, it's not worth thinking about going out there unless we absolutely need to."

From what I've heard so far, it's impossible *not* to think about what's out there. I decide to stop asking about it for the time being.

Soon we arrive at a marshy area. Crickets are chirping and frogs are croaking. The perfectly manicured lawn ends and a path between overgrown plants begins. There are countless ferns, and plants growing different varieties of berries.

Cole points at the path, which seems to be made of peat moss. "This is a bog. It's a neat place to visit to see all sorts of amphibians and cool plants." He motions for me to join him, and jumps up and down a couple of times on the path. "Now you. Jump."

I do as he asks and feel a recoil, like there's a trampoline buried beneath the soil. "It's bouncy."

"That's because there's water just below the surface. If we dug for a few minutes, we'd probably find some."

He steps back onto the lawn and I do the same. "There's lots of mosquitos and some venomous insects in there," he says. "I can lend you some coverings if you want to check it out sometime."

"That would be cool."

"It's best not to explore here alone. You know, just in case."

In case of *what*? Before I can ask, Cole points to where the lawn continues past the bog. "Let me show you where we do our farming and pick our fruit."

We cross the lawn. There isn't much to see in the bog except for wild plants along the border. We pass by three more cabins on the right. The doors to all except one are open.

When we finally pass the edge of the bog, the grassy path we're on opens to a large field. There is more fog on the west side of the Garden. What really piques my curiosity though, is something else.

Between alternating rows of daffodils and tulips is something that seems very out of place—a magnificent spiral staircase. It's as if it was relocated from the foyer of a billionaire's mansion. The steps are made of light marble and the railings are brass-plated.

The peculiarly located staircase isn't the biggest curiosity though. The strangest sight is the low-lying clouds that engulf the top of it. Otherwise, there are only a few scattered clouds high in the sky. This particular puffy segment of cloud cover has somehow been lowered to the top of the staircase. I've never seen anything so odd.

"What's—?"

"It's a staircase," Cole answers bluntly. Then a wide grin spreads across his face. He's poking fun at me.

"I know *that*. Why is it here? Where does it lead? And what's with those clouds?"

I run to the staircase, place one foot on the bottom step and look up. Cole puts a hand on my shoulder.

"Syn, you don't want to go up there."

"It's just so—"

"Weird? Yeah, it is. I don't have an explanation for why it's here. I've been up those stairs and what I witnessed blew my mind. But not everyone has the same experience. Some haven't fared so well up there, so it's best that you admire its wonders from down here."

Because of my CF, I've always been cautious about trying anything new or doing something when the consequences are uncertain. Now I'm feeling more adventurous than ever. Still fixated on the clouds at the top, I have a compelling need to climb the first step, and then another, regardless of Cole's warning. He gently pulls me off the stairs.

"Let's go check out the farm."

He slides his hand down my arm and takes hold of my hand. A shiver goes up my spine. I'm beginning to swoon over a guy who up until an hour ago was a stranger. And I'm not a swooner. At least I wasn't before today.

I reluctantly slide my hand from his grip. Jon didn't hold my hand until our fourth date, and although feeling the touch of Cole's brawny fingers is nice, we did just meet. Regardless of the disappointment on his face, I smile. His smile returns, and we resume our walk across the lawn.

Soon we approach a large area of farmland. Thirteen workers are planting seeds, picking crops, and hoeing the soil. As soon as we come into view, they stop working to observe us; especially to look at *me*. Let me rephrase that: to *stare* at me.

"They don't see a new face around here that often," Cole explains.

He leads me over to a middle-aged Chinese couple kneeling in the dirt.

"This is Syn. Syn, this is Teng and Tian."

I give a friendly wave, feeling shy. They both smile. The man says hello with a strong accent and then they lower their heads and continue to work.

We walk on. "Teng and Tian don't speak much English," Cole says.

Seven other adults are working in the field, along with one kid and three teenagers. Cole doesn't introduce me to all of them, he just waves. They wave back and regard me curiously.

Where the farmland ends, the orchard begins. There's about an acre of land of evenly spaced trees, including apple trees and other varieties of fruit as well. A woman, possibly in her mid-twenties, is standing on a ladder picking fruit. A guy around the same age is raking leaves.

Cole is leading me over to the girl, who hasn't seen us yet, when I notice something and stop. To the right of the orchard are the backs of three cabins. Just beyond the cabins is a pond.

"What's wrong?" Cole asks.

"Um, nothing. Just...is that the pond you found me in?"

"It is."

My pace quickens in the direction of the pond.

"Hey," Cole says, "I was just going to introduce you to a couple of my friends."

I don't respond, determined to move on. Cole catches up with me at one of the cabins and puts his hand on my shoulder. "This cabin's mine."

I shrug and speed past his cabin absentmindedly, coming to a stop at the pond. A tear slides down my cheek.

Cole gently wipes away the tear. "You were floating face down, just over there."

My gaze remains fixed on the water.

"What is it?"

"This pond. It's just like the one in my garden at home." I look up from the water at Cole. "But this isn't my home. Where am I?"

More tears start forming in my eyes. "This doesn't make any sense! Why is this pond just like mine? How did I end up here after falling into the pond back *home*?"

Cole puts his arm around my shoulder. "I don't understand it either. I am glad you ended up here. Otherwise we never would have met."

I look deeply into his eyes—one a soft brown, the other half brown and half cobalt blue. "I'm glad we met too. It's nice here. But I don't know where *here* is. This is so baffling."

A thought suddenly pops into my head. If this pond is just like the one in my garden at home, could there be anything else here that's also similar to home? That could give me some answers. I pull away from Cole and frantically look around. Some of the gardens surrounding the pond appear similar to the ones at home.

And then I see it! The roof of a familiar-looking building jutting above the trees. It's a different color than when I left this morning, but there's no mistaking it. It's my house!

Chapter 7

Home Away from Home

I RUN FOR THE FIRST time since I was a little girl. It seems so easy now. Cole calls out my name, in vain.

There's a pathway leading to the house from the far side of the pond, just like the one in my garden at home. Some of the plants in the garden are similar to the ones at home too. I keep running, and wind my way down the path. More of the house comes into view.

I stop after reaching the end of the path, and look up at the house in its entirety. The structure is gray and built with a combination of wood and red brick. My house is built of red brick too but the outside is mostly white stucco. The wooden stairway leading up to the kitchen on the ground floor is different, possibly rebuilt. But there's no denying it—the structure and shape of the house is identical to mine. I start to feel dizzy.

To the right of the stairway are what look like graves marked with wooden sticks instead of headstones. As I approach the small cemetery, my dizziness swells. I swear there are strange whispers in the air but before I can decipher them, I'm interrupted by Cole.

"What's going on? Why did you run away?"

I close my eyes and shake my head in an attempt to clear it. The whispers stop. The dizziness remains.

"This house... Who lives here?"

Cole avoids the question. "We shouldn't be here."

"Why are you whispering?"

He takes my arm, gently, though I can sense his urgency. "We don't come here, Syn. It's not safe."

"Why not?"

"I don't know. Things happen here. We just avoid it." He tugs on my arm. "Let's go."

"Let's knock on the door and find out who lives here."

Cole looks up at the house and then at me. "You absolutely don't want to do that. You're not from here and don't know how things work."

"Well, then let's walk around to the front. Look around."

"Not now. The sun will be going down soon."

I decide to give him the benefit of the doubt. My mind is clouding up once more and I swear I hear whispers again. Whispers inside my head.

There is definitely something weird about this place.

"Okay," I say quietly. "But promise me you won't stop me from looking around tomorrow."

"All right. Now let's go."

I glance at the house once more, and at the mounds of dirt in the graveyard, and then walk back to the path with Cole. As we put some distance between the house and ourselves, my dizziness dissipates. It's undeniable that there's something frightening about that house, and yet I'm not scared enough to stay away.

We walk in silence for a few minutes, until I speak up. "Who's buried there?"

"I don't know. Maybe no one. Those could just be sticks in the ground."

He isn't being honest with me. He knows something.

The sun is getting lower and Aunt Ruth comes to mind. I should have tried to find a way home instead of taking a tour. Perhaps feeling healthy made me selfish. Surely, my aunt will understand when I tell her about this place.

"Is there any way to reach someone from here? Phone? Internet?"

"I'm afraid we don't have either. Even our electricity is limited."

I sigh. "How will I get home?"

"You don't like it here?"

"I do. I like it a lot. I can't stay forever though. There are people back home who must be worried sick about me. The longer I stay, the more worried they'll be."

Cole can't hide the disappointment on his face. "Honestly, I don't know how to get you home. You said the pond I found you in is similar to the pond you fell into at home, right?"

"I didn't fall. I was pushed. But yeah."

"Maybe there's something connecting the two places. If we swim to the bottom, perhaps we can find something."

"Okay. I sigh again. "I do feel really good being here, by the way."

"I feel really good having you here too."

"Hopefully my aunt doesn't go too crazy worrying about me." As I listen to myself say this, I realize how ridiculous it sounds. Of course she's already called the police.

"Let me talk to some people, see if they have any ideas about how you might get home. If we can figure out how, maybe you could go back and forth. Maybe we could come see you too."

How amazing would that be? If I could live my life at home with my aunt and come here when I'm really ill. How perfect! Literally, having the best of both worlds.

"If you could ask around, that would be great," I say as we walk up to Rose's cabin. "It would be great if I could go back and forth, and have you visit me."

Cole cups his hand over mine and smiles.

"And tomorrow, we'll go and check out the house?"

He pulls his hand away. "Yeah. If you insist. I'd still advise against it."

"Okay, good. Thanks so much for today."

"You're very welcome. "

The door opens and Rose's face peeks out. "There you are. Did you have a nice tour of the Garden?"

"I did. Is your offer still open for me to stay the night?"

"Of course! Stay as long as you like. Flint and I were just about to have a bite and there's more than enough for the two of you."

"Thanks Rose," Cole says, "but I'll be heading off now. Good night."

"Night, Cole." I enter the cabin with Rose.

Flint is sitting at the kitchen table, where there are three dishes of food arranged—pasta with a creamy white sauce and either basil or parsley sprinkled on top, a bowl of potatoes, and a plate of steamed vegetables. There's also a glass pitcher of water with some lemon slices floating at the top. Considering that I don't usually get excited about eating, I'm surprised by my hunger, just from looking at the food and taking in its aroma.

Flint raises a hand to greet me.

"Hi, Flint."

"Flint, do you mind getting another plate and some utensils for Syn?" Rose asks as she rearranges the table to make room. "And a glass."

"Let me help," I offer.

"I can do it." Flint gets up and goes into the next room. Rose pulls out a chair for me and lights a couple of candles.

"I made sure to make enough food in case we had guests," she says. "I'm so happy you're staying with us."

The food is as delicious as it looks, and it's nice to enjoy a meal without struggling to digest it. I'm curious about where they get their food though. Growing potatoes and vegetables would be easy, but... "I was wondering where you get some of the food. Like the pasta and the sauce. Do you make it here?"

Rose and Flint exchange a long look before Rose answers sharply. "We have limited resources in the Garden. When supplies are low some of the men go into the fog to gather more."

"Oh." I don't understand how you'd get ingredients for creamy pasta sauce from fog, but the subject seems to be a touchy one. "This all tastes very good."

When I ask to help Rose and Flint clear the dirty dishes Rose insists that they take care of it. As the dishes clank in the kitchen sink, I peer out the window from the living room. The sun is nearly down. There is a clock on the table by the bed I woke up in this morning. The time is 7:54. I usually don't eat dinner this late at home.

Flint appears, though Rose is still clanking away in the kitchen.

"Is there anything I can do?" I offer again.

"No," Flint says. "My mom is almost done." He sits down on the couch.

"What do you do at night? I don't see a TV."

"What's a TV?" Flint asks.

Yes, some families don't have televisions, but to not even know what a TV is? Strange. He's amazed at the prospect after listening to my explanation.

"Mom, why don't we have a TV?" he asks when Rose joins us.

"TVs need power to make them work, Honey. Remember that we have limited power."

"Right," Flint says, disappointed.

Rose suggests we play a game. She fetches three board games: Clue, Scrabble, and Battleship. I don't ask where they got them; from the mysterious fog, no doubt. Flint is excited to play Battleship so we go with that. Rose and I play as a team as it's a two-player game. Flint is confident that he can beat us. I've never played before. It's kind of lame but they seem to enjoy themselves. Sticking plastic pegs into toy boats is pretty primitive when you've grown up playing games on your laptop and phone.

After we're done (Flint won, as he predicted), Rose tells Flint he should get ready for bed. I help Rose gather the game pieces.

"Flint goes to bed at nine," she says, "If you'd like to stay up later, you can stay in my room until you're ready to go to sleep."

"That's okay. I'm pretty tired."

Rose nods and bounces to her feet. My aunt, who must be around the same age, would be moaning from muscle pains after sitting cross-legged on the floor for so long. Rose puts the game on the bedside table and hands me a folded nightgown.

"Lily dropped this by earlier. It should fit nicely."

"That was nice of her."

"She'd like to get to know you better. There aren't too many kids her age here."

Rose neatens up the room and lays a blanket on the bed. I get cleaned up in the washroom and when I push open the door, Flint is standing in front of the mirror, wearing only his underwear. I jump backwards in surprise at the unusual sight before me.

Most of Flint's back is covered in green scales, like a lizard or a crocodile. Even stranger, a reptilian tail is tucked into his underwear.

He screams when he sees my reflection and quickly pulls a towel over his body and spins around. I cover my eyes in embarrassment and shock.

Rose rushes into the room. "Shit. I really wish you hadn't seen that."

Chapter 8

A Strange Tail

ROSE HURRIES ACROSS THE ROOM. It seems like she's going to attack.

"I'm so sorry. I didn't think anyone was in there."

She brushes past me. Flint puts his pajama bottoms on and runs into his mom's open arms.

"Sorry, Mom," he says in a squeaky voice. "I should have locked the door."

"That's okay, Sweetie. You're not used to having someone else here."

As Rose turns around, I sense malice in her eyes. Then I realize it's actually concern. She lets go of Flint, grips both my arms, and stares into my eyes. "Syn, this is very important. You cannot, for any reason, tell anyone what you saw a moment ago."

"Okay. I won't."

"Please. This is *extremely* important. Don't mention this to *anyone*, even friends. People talk and this must not get out. Things could get bad for Flint and me."

"I promise, Rose. I'm not sure about what I just saw and nobody would believe me anyway. Besides, it's none of my business. Don't worry, I won't tell a soul. Ever."

Rose hugs me tightly. "You're an angel," she says, her voice heaving. "Thank you."

Flint, now wearing a pajama top too, comes over and hugs us both. For the first time since waking up here, I feel a sense of belonging. These people are like family, which is crazy because we barely know each other. As strange as it is, I really don't care why Flint has scales and a tail. I always hated it when people asked me questions about my illness, and so I promise myself to not ask even one more question about Flint's unusual appearance. That said, this entire place is strange. So many things are different from my home. I mean, Cole has two faces!

When Flint is done in the washroom, I go in. He barely acknowledges me, so I smile to show him I'm still a friend. A few seconds after I enter the washroom, Rose pops her head in.

"If you'd like a bath, feel free to take one."

"That's okay. I'll take one in the morning."

She hands me a brand-new toothbrush. It's an Oral-B; the same brand Aunt Ruth buys. They use Crest toothpaste. Am I in some other world or in the U.S.? If I'm in the same country—the same world—how come people can live forever here?

I brush my teeth, then shut the door and use the toilet. After dressing in the nightgown Rose gave me, I walk into the next room. Rose is sitting on the edge of the couch beside Flint. She stands up and tosses a blanket into the air, and when it lands, tucks it into the cracks of the couch.

"Are you sure you don't want to sleep in your bed, Flint?" I ask. "I don't mind sleeping on the couch."

"I like it here," he replies.

Rose leans down and kisses Flint on the forehead, then leads me to a chair in the kitchen where there is a pile of folded clothes. "Here are some fresh clothes from Lily."

"Thanks."

"Is there anything else I can get you?"

"Do you have any books? Something to read before bed?"

"There are a few books in the other room. Let me get you something."

"I'm glad you're here with us, Syn," Flint says as I get into the freshly made bed.

My heart melts a little. "I'm glad I'm here too."

Rose returns with three battered paperbacks; unfamiliar science fiction—*The Day of the Triffids*, *The Crystal Worlds*, and *Stranger in a Strange Place*. Though I can identify with the title of the last one, they're not exactly my genre of choice.

"We're a little limited with what we have to read," Rose says as if in reply to my inner thoughts. Someone else might have something better."

"Thank you."

Rose says good night and leaves the room.

Flint says "Good night, Syn," and rolls over to face the back of the couch.

I pick up one of the books, flip through its yellowed pages and put it back on the table. I'm ready to go to sleep anyway and reach over to flick off the light. The light in the next room goes out a few minutes later.

The room is not pitch-black even though there are no cabins or street lights nearby; the light from the full moon reflects through the window.

The clock on the table reads 9:34. My normal bedtime is usually after 10:30. I always have trouble sleeping, knowing I have to get up early to take meds and put on my physical therapy vest. It still boggles my mind that I won't have to do that here.

While lying in bed staring up at the ceiling, the day's events run through my mind. Who would believe that a terminally ill girl would find a garden that grants eternal life? Everything feels so real but I still half-expect to wake up tomorrow in my own bed at home, hacking up mucus and feeling like my lungs are on fire.

The people I've met have been so warm and inviting; Rose and Flint. And then Cole; his appearance may be odd, yet there's something about him that is immensely (dare I say it?) sexy. He's kind. Strong. He seems to have feelings for me too. The Garden isn't teeming with girls his age, although I wonder what relationships he's had. Perhaps with Lily?

Everything here is so weird and new. There has to be a way for me to get home, even if it doesn't happen immediately. So, the last thing I need to think about is a boy.

I roll over on my side, rest my hand under my face, close my eyes and immediately picture Janna. There is no way to know if my dear friend is still alive. It makes me extremely sad to think that she may be gone. If she were in better shape and had longer, perhaps there would be a way to bring her here. I could bring Aunt Ruth and Janna's mom and they could live in this magical place with us forever. Tears trickle onto my pillow.

The next thing I know, I'm being shaken awake. Sure enough, I'm in my bed at home. But my chest feels fine and there's no mucus buildup in my lungs. I rub my eyes and instead of seeing my aunt like expected, Cole is standing over me. He looks extremely concerned.

"I told you not to come here. It's not safe."

"This is my home."

"This isn't *your* home, Syn. It's *her* home. And the last thing you want is for *her* to find you here."

I blink and open my eyes again. Yes, still in Rose's cabin. Flint is asleep on the couch. It was just a dream—or if this whole place is a dream, it was a dream within a dream.

Who was Cole was talking about? The person who lives in my house? Could he have meant the house here? The one that looks like my place back home? Why was he so concerned? Will he come up with an excuse to keep me from going there again?

I sit up and check the time. 4:35 A.M. I feel rested, and why not? I've had about as much sleep as usual. I quietly stand up and walk to the window. Not a blade of grass is moving. There are no sounds other than the squeaking of the wooden floor under my bare feet.

I have an idea. Daring, but inviting nonetheless. I can sneak out and have a look around that house while everyone is asleep. I should be able to find my way to the pond and from there follow the path. The full moon will provide enough light.

I creep over to the clothes Rose set out and get dressed carefully. There are no socks and no sign of my shoes. So, in bare feet I tiptoe to the door, almost holding my breath. Just as my fingers reach to unhook the chain, there is a whisper behind me.

"Where are you going?" asks Flint. "Are you leaving us?"

Chapter 9

The Woman in the Iron Mask

THE SORROW IN FLINT'S EYES breaks my heart. We've known each other less than a day and he's already so attached. Thoughts about leaving this place make me feel even sadder.

"Don't worry, I'll be back." My whisper seems loud in this stillness.

"Where are you going?"

There's no harm in telling him the truth, is there? "To see that big house."

His look of sorrow abruptly changes to worry. And fear. "That's not a good idea."

"This is something I need to do," I tell him. "I won't be long. Promise."

"Wait a sec." Flint scurries off.

I'm afraid he's going to wake up his mom. Instead, he returns with a silver flashlight. "Use this. So you can find your way. Don't use it around the house. She might see you."

"Who might see me?"

Fear returns to the boy's eyes. He scans the room behind him, as if afraid someone might be listening. "Be careful," is all he can say.

I shut the door behind me without making a sound. It's chilly and the dew on the grass is colder on my feet than expected. Although the Garden is dark, the moonlight brightens the path. After sliding the flashlight into a pocket, I walk in the direction of the pond. Soon, my body heats up and the cold no longer bothers me. Crickets are chirping and there is the odd rustle of a bird or squirrel in the trees. The moonlight reflecting off the water is almost magical.

There is a cabin on my left, with no lights on. They are as sound asleep as I should be. Cole's cabin is just up ahead. I begin to tiptoe past it and hear someone walking behind me. Barely stopping myself from yelping I spin around, hoping to see Cole. I let out a sigh of relief as my eyes focus on a gray rabbit sitting on the grass. It looks my way and then hops off.

Feeling composed again, my bare feet carry me onward. The sky is clear, illuminated by an expansive blanket of stars. Though the location of this Garden is unknown to me, it's comforting to believe that I am underneath the same stars that watch over my home.

While slipping past a third darkened cabin, the feeling that I'm being watched tenses every one of my muscles. This is the same feeling I often have back at home when walking to and from school. Once past the cabin, I turn on the flashlight and shine the beam around me. There isn't anyone to be seen. It's probably just my nerves, or paranoia, as usual.

There is suddenly cold concrete under my feet and the pond ends abruptly. I deliberate turning around and returning to Rose's cabin, and trying this tomorrow night with shoes and a warm coat. But who knows what the day will bring? If I end up going home before coming back here, I'll never stop wondering about the similarities between this house and my own. Determined, I continue walking across the hard concrete, reaching the cemetery and the back of the house in a few minutes.

The graves pique my curiosity, although just like before my mind turns to mush while standing near them. Hugging the side of the house so nobody can see me, I decide to go around the other way and check out the graves on my way back. My head becomes clearer the farther away I get from the graves. It still seems like there are words whispering inside my head, but they are difficult to decipher.

While sliding my body alongside the exterior of the house toward the carport, I wonder if my aunt's car is parked there. That would totally freak me out. However, after coming around the corner, I see nothing but blackness. I turn on the flashlight. The empty carport looks like the one at home. Eerie. At home, there's a rectangular basement window on the wall. This window is boarded up.

Time to check out the front of the house. At home, there's a modest-sized garden next to the driveway, between the street and my house, and across the street are several large estates, mostly farms. Here, there's just a narrow road and a wall of fog; the same fog that Cole told me to stay out of. The same fog that seems to send a chill down Rose's spine whenever the subject comes up.

The only way to get a good view of the house is from the front lawn. I turn off the flashlight and move onto the soft, moist grass, a welcome relief for my sore feet. Backing up on the grassy cushion, I look up. The color and building materials are different but the shape of the structure is identical to my house. Identical to the house that's been in my family for over a century.

Fearing my presence might have been noticed, my eyes dart to the windows. They're covered with either wooden shutters or curtains, and yet it still feels like I'm being watched. I spin around in a full circle. No one's there. There could be someone in the fog, but it's too thick to see through and using the flashlight isn't a good idea. The feeling of being watched isn't going away and I warm to the idea of cutting my expedition short.

While heading to the house, I am stopped in my tracks by a distinctive creaking sound. My head spins around to face the wooden front steps and the door they lead to. Nothing. Yep—being out here is creeping me out big time. It's time to get out of here. Taking a closer look at the gravestones is absolutely out of the question. I bolt past the side of the house, ignoring the pain from my sore feet, fixated on the covered windows and watching for any sign of movement. No one is there.

Behind the house, I find myself at the cemetery again. My head immediately clouds up. Worse than before. Words are trying to articulate themselves inside my mind. My head is pounding. I fall to my knees, dropping the flashlight, covering my ears. Pounding. Voices! Can't think straight. Words are whispering inside my head, louder now, clearer. *Wren! Wren way! Hey!* No, that's not it. Pushing past the pain. Forcing myself to concentrate. Listen. Harder! The flurry of whispers escalates, intensifies. Words now. *Run! Run away! Hurry!*

My eyes fly open. The cloudiness has subsided. I stand up. Finding out who that warning was from doesn't matter right now. What is important is to get the hell out of here! And yet, my feet are rooted to the spot, my eyes glued to a second-floor window. The curtain is no longer drawn. A woman is standing there. She has short hair and is wearing a mask. A thick, metal mask with uneven holes that reveal her eyes staring down at me. Her lips twist into a sinister smile as she withdraws into the darkness of the house.

Stumbling, I grab the flashlight, accidently flicking it on, and run as fast as my feet will carry me. The beam lands on two creatures squatting to the left of me. If the light wasn't shining on them, I would say they were large dogs. Alas, these creatures are covered with shiny green scales, similar to the patch of skin on Flint's back. They have a head that resembles a dog except for their snouts, which extend like a crocodile's. Long, heavy tongues are hanging out of their panting mouths. Long tails vibrate and crackle like a rattle-snake's. They growl at me, baring razer-like teeth. Drool rains from their mouths.

The whispers promptly return. Louder and louder. *Run! Run away! Hurry!* I do just that, with the terrifying beasts right on my tail.

Chapter 10

The Girl Who Wasn't There

I SPRINT AS FAST AS possible, surprised by my speed. At home, breathlessness from walking at a brisk pace was normal. Now, my legs function like they're bionic limbs.

Despite this speed, the growling behind me intensifies. At the pond, my feet slip on the dewy grass, my arms flailing to regain balance. A searing pain tears up my calf as one of the creatures punctures my flesh with its razor teeth. My body lands with a thud on the wet grass. I try to get up and collapse again. Scaly claws grip my back. I'm done for.

"Stay!"

I twist my head around, roll onto my back. Standing behind the panting creatures is a young girl, about nine or ten years old, slim, with brown hair. The pale moonlight reveals a startling resemblance…to me!

She gazes into the eyes of the creatures. They are instantly transfixed, as if they have fallen under a magician's spell. "Go home!" she demands, pointing in the direction of the house. Relieved, I watch the creatures scurry away, then turn to the girl who saved my life. She is gone.

I stagger to my feet, wincing from the pain in my calf. There is absolutely no sign of the girl. It's like she vanished. Who is she? Why does she look so much like me? How was she able to control those creatures? What *were* those scary-as-hell things? And who was that sinister, smiling woman in the window? So many unanswered questions. I sigh.

Surprisingly, the bite on my leg isn't too bad. Some skin is torn but as sharp as those teeth looked, I'm shocked it's not a lot worse. It's a bit sore to touch, though not nearly as painful as a moment ago. Does this strange place heal physical injuries too?

During the return walk to Rose's cabin, the pain magically fades away. Knowing that the sun will rise in less than an hour, I quicken my pace. I must get home before anyone sees me. Cole's cabin is just as quiet as it was before. He warned me. I should have waited for him to take me to the house during the day. Not being familiar with this place, I need to start listening to the people who are.

After arriving back at the cabin, I open the door as quietly as possible and go inside. Flint is sound asleep. Good. I close the door behind me carefully and lay down on the bed, not even bothering to change my clothes or wipe off my dirty feet. It's just after 5:30 A.M. A vision of the girl who saved me from those creatures comes to mind. Her big brown eyes are staring at me. Immediately, my lids flutter closed as if her eyes have placed me into a peaceful trance.

At 11:12 A.M. I wake, squinting at the brilliant sunshine glaring through the windows and quite surprised that I slept so late; the first time in my entire short life. I stretch my arms and then drop my feet onto the floor. There are grass stains on the sheets from my dirty feet. Regret for not cleaning up churns inside my stomach.

The couch is empty. "Hello?" My voice is loud enough for someone in the next room to hear. There is no reply. The bite on my calf has completely healed, with no trace of a scar or even so much as a scratch; it's like the bite never even happened. If it weren't for the fact that I'm still dressed and have grass-stained heels, the whole experience could have been just a dream…well, more like a nightmare actually.

I tiptoe to the door, trying not to dirty the floor with my feet. Other than birds celebrating the beautiful day with their sweet melodies, there is no sight or sound of anyone or anything. Maybe Rose and Flint are at the Square.

When I arrive at the Square there aren't any tables set up. Lily and another girl are standing by the well next to a wheelbarrow piled high with a mountain of fruits and vegetables. The girl beside Lily is a few years younger than me, thirteen perhaps, with gorgeous caramel-colored skin. Her face lights up as she sees me approaching the well.

Lily gives me the once-over. I didn't check myself out in the mirror before leaving the house and must surely look like a mess. I bet my hair is a disaster and my clothes are wrinkled from sleeping in them.

"Hey, Syn," Lily says. "Glad to see the clothes fit."

"Thanks for lending them to me."

"No worries." Lily motions to the other girl. "This is my friend, Nell. Nell, this is Syn."

Nell gives me a big, unexpected hug. It takes me a moment to squeeze back because she catches me off guard.

"I've heard so much about you!" she says. "It's not often we see a new face here."

"So I've heard."

"I can get you more clothes," Lily says. "There is lots of stuff I almost never wear."

"Thanks. I'm not sure how long I'll be staying here though."

Nell frowns. "You just got here."

"There are people at home who will be worried sick about me." And there are things here that…" I pause, trying to find the right words, really wanting to say, "Things that scare me." Instead, my sentence trails off and dies.

Lily bends down and picks up a towel from a pile on the ground. "Have a seat," she says. "Your feet look gross." She pours some well water on the towel, wrings it out and hands it to me.

I wipe off the grass and dirt stains as best as I can. The dirt comes off but the grass stains are stubborn.

"So, you went out last night to do some exploring," Lily says.

"How do you know that?"

"Rose told me."

"Is she mad?"

"No, of course not. The Garden is a very quiet and peaceful place. People rarely get mad about anything. Things are pretty much perfect here."

"Some things about last night are far from peaceful or perfect."

"Well, silly, when you start exploring a place you don't know at night when everyone else is asleep, what do you expect? Do you walk around at night where you live?"

"Well, no. But at home there wouldn't be crocodile-dog hybrids chasing me. Or voices whispering in my head. Or—"

"Shhh," Nell hushes. She and Lily glance around nervously, making me think they don't want anyone to overhear. We all stand up at the same time.

"Why don't you help us clean the produce?" Lily suggests.

Lily and Nell seem nice, but cleaning fruit and having girl talk is the last thing on my mind. I return the towel to Lily. "I'm feeling kind of gross and want to take a shower. But I'd like to catch up later."

"Okay," Lily says. "I'll be here with my mom this afternoon."

"Oh, wait a minute..." There is one burning question that needs to be answered. I'm pretty certain about the response I will get but some more clarity is worth a shot. "Um, do either of you know who lives in the big house?"

Their expressions freeze. They say nothing. I decide to prod them some more. "Does a woman live there? A woman wearing some sort of metal mask?"

Their stunned faces glance at each other, a hint of fear flickering in their eyes; regret about bringing it up in mine.

"You should go take that shower," Lily says. "We'll see you later. Okay?" She and Nell turn and walk toward the wheelbarrow.

Why don't they want to talk about the house or that woman? Or the creatures? Yeah, they're scary, but what's the harm in talking? They obviously know something.

No one is home at Rose's cabin. In no time at all, I get into the bathtub, turn on the tap and pull the metal peg to turn on the shower. The water is only mildly warm, yet soothing. With memories of last night shelved, my mind clears. Meditation is new to me but this is what people who meditate must aim for. It would be nice to take that bath Rose and I talked about last night, and to get rid of these stubborn grass stains, although it's questionable just how much water they have, since they wash all their fruit with well water. After letting the water rain over my body and soothe my soul for a few minutes, I take the soap and shampoo (both well-known brands), give myself a quick scrub and shut off the shower.

After drying off, thoughts start to seep back. Not about what happened last night, however. More specifically, about the house. And about the pond. And this entire mysterious place. I get dressed in clean clothes and walk to the front room, deciding to draw a map. There is a pad of paper and a pencil in a drawer. I grab one of the books Rose gave me last night, sit on the couch and place the book on my lap under the paper. In geography class, drawing maps was something I excelled at. As long as I can recall where everything is, this should be easy.

First, I start with the house, which is around the middle of the north side of the Garden. I draw the wall of fog in front. Then, I draw the fog that borders the gardens first and fill in the rest of the map. Clearly, I will need more than one sheet of paper to include everything in the Garden.

I rip off the piece of paper from the pad, crumple it up, and throw it onto my bed. Recycling is an obsession at home, but it's doubtful there's a recycling facility here. I walk over to the table by the window and rip off a new sheet of paper from the pad, then another and another. Nine in total. When spread out, the sheets practically cover the table. I border the map with the fog, and draw and label all of the places I have explored—the house, the pond, the orchard, the farm, the bog, the cabins, and the Square.

When I'm finished, I tuck the pencil behind my ear and stare at the map thoughtfully. Then, taking the pencil from behind my ear, I draw a circle around the land the house is on, part of the path in front of the house where I stood looking up at the windows, the garden area below, the pond, and a little more. Other parts of the land are eventually circled, but it's the large circle at the top that interests me most.

"Hey, Sweetie."

Being so deep in thought, I didn't notice someone had walked into the room. I turn around and smile.

"Hi Rose."

"So, you're thinking about finding a way home."

Surprised that Rose didn't ask about my sneaking out last night, I stare at the map and say in a low voice, mostly to myself, "In a way I'm not sure I ever really left."

Chapter 11

Stairway to Heaven

"WHAT DID YOU SAY?" Rose asks.

"Oh, uh, nothing."

She leans over my shoulder to study the map. "That's the Garden."

"It is." I smile and start stacking each sheet of paper, numbering them so they can easily be reassembled.

"You're welcome to keep those there," Rose says, "as long as we move them before dinner."

"Thanks. I'll put them away for now."

I place the sheets of paper on the table beside my bed, using one of Rose's books as a paper-weight.

"You know you're welcome to stay here as long as you'd like, Syn," says Rose from behind me.

I turn around to meet her gaze.

"If you want to stay in the Garden and would rather not share a place, we can get you set up in a tent for a while. We could even build you a cabin."

This *is* awkward. My desire to go home should be self-explanatory. The need to go back—or at least the feeling I *should* go back—is an important statement considering that living here would be forever and that I'd die in a few short years at home. Gee, when I put it like that, I admit my desire to leave is a bit strange.

"Thanks Rose. I really appreciate it. I'm going to go for a walk." I brush past her, heading to the door.

"Why don't I join you?"

"Some time alone would be nice, if you don't mind." I smile, open the door and close it behind me, not giving Rose time to try to convince me otherwise. Talking to anyone right now—even Cole—is out of the question.

The beauty of the Garden is undeniable. Like my garden at home, it's a paradise. But my garden at home is just that though, a garden. This Garden is a community, possibly their entire world. It's beautiful. However, it's also full of mystery. And danger.

The pond is not far away. I pass Cole's cabin and walk for another minute so he won't be able to see me if he comes outside. The lily pads might be floating in different spots but otherwise this pond is identical to mine. Plus, the entire area circled at the top of the map I drew is a clone of my property at home. I'm certain of it.

There is nobody around except for a white rabbit sniffing the grass behind me. I stroll alongside the pond. Everything looks so familiar. It wouldn't be too much of a surprise if Aunt Ruth appeared from out of nowhere and asked where I've been.

My path takes me back to that house. There is no movement at the window where the masked woman appeared last night. The curtains are drawn. My dizziness returns. Thankfully, there aren't any whispering voices this time. Quickening my pace to get away from the graves, I walk along the back of the house, past the empty carport to the orchard. The dizziness subsides. Those creatures might not be outside when the sun is out, but it's not worth sticking around and taking any chances.

Voices in the orchard alert me to the presence of three strangers. I skirt around the trees and creep through the back of the orchard, hoping to remain invisible. A wide-open grassy space with a circular rose garden in the center presents itself, the wall of fog looming in the background. This fog…it's in every direction! My assumptions and the map drawn this morning are bang on. The Garden forms a rectangular shape bordered by this misty wall.

On to the farm. There are more voices. Real voices. Every muscle freezes, my ears strain to hear more but it's impossible to make out what is being said. One of the voices is definitely Cole's though. I hide behind the trunk of a giant old apple tree, slide down onto my knees and bury my head in my arms. A heavy breath releases with a sigh of exasperation.

The map is most puzzling. Why is this area so similar to my family's property back home, yet the areas around it are so different? Where I am sitting right now would be the McNeils' property. They have a huge house and a free-range chicken farm. At my insistence, Aunt Ruth stopped buying eggs from the supermarket, because those chickens are inhumanely crammed into cages. Aunt Ruth buys only what I call "happy chicken" eggs from the McNeils. Even with the discount they give us, the eggs are almost three dollars more for a dozen than the "miserable chicken" eggs but it's worth it. The yolks are a richer orange color and my aunt can't argue because they taste better too.

However, here there is no house. No barns. No chickens. Certainly no McNeils. If I go home and never return, this will bug me for the rest of my short life. Mysteries drive me nuts. I crave answers. After clearing my head, I stand up. There is no sound of Cole, just a couple of female voices. And a sound from the sky. An airplane is flying overhead. There is a United Airlines logo on the side of it.

While scurrying to the west end of the Garden, my pace slows upon approaching the wall of fog.

Cole warned me about going into the fog. No argument here. It's eerie as hell. It's so thick. I can't see anything through it. Cool air emits from the gray mist and fear that something will reach out and pull me in takes hold. From what I've experienced in this place so far, that doesn't seem so farfetched at all.

I move along the wall of the fog (making sure not to stand too close), and head onto the farm. There are eight people working but I only recognize Teng and Tian, the Chinese couple Cole introduced me to. A woman yells "Hi there!" Pretending not to hear, I keep walking, briskly crossing the farmland.

Another plane roars overhead. This place isn't so isolated after all. I must be in the same world I came from or at least in a world connected to that world. But what's on the other side of the fog? How will it be possible to find out without going into it?

Not long after leaving the farm, my intended destination appears in front of me—the peculiar spiral staircase that disappears up into a mysterious low-lying cloud. Cole told me that it's better to climb the stairs with someone, but waiting is not an option. Climbing to the top might let me see where the planes go after passing by the Garden.

I glance back to make sure no one is watching and then run up the staircase, circling around three times before stopping directly underneath the cloud. A light mist brushes my cheeks. Nervously holding my breath, I step up into the cloud.

There are more steps inside the cloud and during my climb it's impossible to see anything. As my head rises through the top of the cloud, my path takes me off the stairs and onto a flat platform. I'm now standing on a large, circular balcony surrounded by a metal railing. Something in my stomach doesn't sit right but a strange impulse invites me to walk to the railing and look down. The sight below is unbelievable!

The Garden is visible in its entirety but rather than being a couple of stories up like I should be, it's like looking at it from way up in the clouds.

The Garden appears just as it was drawn on my map. The wall of fog borders the whole Garden and there's no way out except through it. Unfortunately, this bird's-eye view doesn't reveal what's on the other side of the fog. The Garden is surrounded by what seems like infinite walls of fog. There is *nothing* else as far as I can see.

The roar of the plane that just flew past is much louder than when listening from the ground. It's flying over the flat ceiling of endless fog. The scary thing is, it's actually at my level, like my body is floating in the sky behind it.

Suddenly, something flashes through the fog. There's another flash. Then another. Like a strobe light is beaming up from below.

As an avalanche of questions rushes through my mind, that strange feeling in my stomach moves into my chest; something not felt since just before arriving at this place. Mucus is rapidly building up in my lungs and throat. The coughing begins. Then the hacking. Falling to my knees, a feeling of dread encompasses me. Common symptoms of my cystic fibrosis are rushing back all at once, and even worse, there's no medicine or doctors up here... or in the Garden for that matter—nobody is *supposed* to get sick! If I don't do something quick, I won't live to see tomorrow.

Chapter 12

Along Came...a Spider?!

MY HANDS AND KNEES SCRAPE against the coarse surface of the platform and my desperate lungs wheeze and rattle as my symptoms rapidly worsen. A number of minutes are spent coughing up phlegm. The last time this happened, my doctor admitted me to the hospital and kept me there for three weeks.

I have to get my head together and do something quickly. Everything was fine a few moments ago so the properties up here must be different from the Garden below. I reach out. Grab hold of the railing. Try to stand up. Snot trickles from my nose as my shaky arms strain to hoist me up again. Feeling faint from dizziness, either because of the altitude, the sudden return of my illness or both, I squint at the ground far below. It doesn't matter how far away it is. I use all my remaining strength to drag myself to the stairs.

My fingers grasp the handrail while my feet stumble down the stairs and then, disappear into the cloud. While descending beneath the white mist, it's apparent that I'm just a few stories above the ground like I should be. Encouraged, but still coughing, I painstakingly make my way down.

The ground is only four steps below when there is a thump in my chest—no pain, just a thump. The surprise makes me lose my footing. I tumble down the stairs and fall face down onto the grass. Lying there for a short moment, I take in comforting, fresh aromas and the feeling of warm grass tickling my face. Then, I flip over onto my back with so much more ease than was possible just a few moments ago.

My coughing has ceased and while I'm lying on the grass marveling at the beautiful clear blue sky, my lungs are clearing up. Breathing comes naturally. The staircase beckons again. It is as if I had climbed the Tower of Babel, built to reach the heavens. It makes little sense.

After a few more minutes pass I feel a hundred percent better, yet have no urge to stand up. Still gazing at the sky, I wonder what would have happened if I had died up there. Or what if I just stayed here forever? My aunt will live on, probably believing my disappearance was the result of an abduction; never knowing the truth. If I die from my disease at home, she can have closure. Not knowing what has happened to me would haunt her forever. Aunt Ruth and I may not have the tightest relationship, but we love each other. I'm all she has and often wonder what she will do without me. It breaks my heart even more to think of her concern that I might have been held captive, or killed and thrown into a ditch.

Surprisingly, my next thought is of Ebby. What she must be going through. Even though in my opinion we're more companions than friends, she believes otherwise. Ebby sees me as a close friend and realizing this makes me feel pretty low, like I've only been using her for company while she truly cares for me. It surprises me that I care so much about how Ebby must be feeling. And that my thoughts went to her before Janna.

As much as it pains me, even if Janna is still hanging on, the girl I love like a sister is no longer a part of my life. But she will remain in my heart forever. I wipe tears from my eyes and force myself to get up. It's important to find Cole. *Now.* He has to help me find a way home as soon as possible. Maybe I'll bring Aunt Ruth here, or at least make sure she knows where I am. Ebby too. But staying here any longer would be selfish.

I walk through the farm and then the orchards, careful to avoid everyone. Making small talk is not a priority. Strangers smile and wave, like I'm a celebrity visiting their village. Getting close. Through the orchard. To Cole's place. The walk is pleasant this time, as I pay more attention to the fresh scents, beautiful blossoms, and birds chirping. I take my time.

Cole's door is wide open. I stand at the door and peek inside. His cabin is the same size as Rose's, with the same layout. The main room is set up as a living space. Furnishings are minimal—just a couch, kitchen table, a couple of chairs, and a lamp. There are no decorations of any kind. It barely even looks lived in.

I knock on the door. No answer. There's no one in sight anywhere. Although there is a voice in my head telling me otherwise, it should be okay to go inside if the door is open. Right?

It is darker here than in Rose's cabin because the windows are facing a different direction. I walk through the spartan living room and poke my head through the doorway. The next room has a small kitchen like Rose's, and a bed. Rose has a lot of cooking accessories and a variety of seasonings. In this room there is only a pot and salt and pepper shakers. The cupboards beneath the countertop are filled with plenty of pots, containers, and such. For a young guy, he sure keeps everything organized.

Next to his freshly made bed is a night table with a lamp, a box of tissues, and a framed picture of a young couple and a little boy—a boy whose face is divided like Cole's. It's tempting to snoop in the night table drawers but an inner voice reminds me that I know better. Turning around to leave, I notice the light is on under the washroom door.

Could Cole be home? While I'm snooping in his cabin?

When the toilet flushes, I dart to the next room and through the front door, breathless. What was I thinking? Back at home, it never would have occurred to me to walk into a neighbor's house, even if the door was open.

"Hey," Cole says from behind.

His voice startles me. I jump and spin around with an expression surely laced with guilt. Telling the truth is the only way out. "Sorry to intrude. I've been looking for you."

Cole grins. "That's fine. We're pretty friendly around here. If someone's door is open, they don't mind visitors coming inside."

"Guess that's why it seemed okay to come in."

"You're starting to feel comfortable here. Good. Maybe you'll decide to stay?"

Spending more time with Cole would be great, but staying isn't an option. "That's why I came to talk to you."

"Oh? I was hoping maybe you just missed me."

"That too." My smile is flirtatious, which is so unlike me. Though it doesn't take long before I remember the serious nature of my intent. "Cole, I really need to get home. People there must be worried sick by now."

Cole is disappointed. "Understood. But honestly, unless we can figure out how you got here, it's going to be hard to get you back."

That's not what I needed to hear. "I was pushed into the pond at home. And ended up in the pond here."

"That's right. We could swim to the bottom and see what we find. I'd like to run this idea by some of the others, okay?"

"Okay. But quickly, all right? I need to go home as soon as possible."

"Sure," Cole replies. His tone is casual, which makes me think he doesn't truly understand the urgency.

"Could you talk to them now?" I plead.

"Like *right now*? I was hoping we could go for a walk."

Cole takes my hand and a tingle runs through my body. I tug my hand free and move away. He needs to take this more seriously.

"Maybe later. After you talk to some people about finding me a way home."

Cole frowns but nods. "Sure. I'll take a rain check on that walk."

"Okay."

He closes the door and walks off in the direction of the orchard. I go to check out the spot where Cole said he found me in the pond. Two ducks are paddling in the water, dipping their heads occasionally to eat bugs. Frogs are croaking somewhere out of view.

I sigh, hoping Cole will keep his promise. It might be worth taking off my sandals and jumping into the pond right now. Maybe a white glow will take me home. A comforting vision of Aunt Ruth waiting on the other side with a towel, and rushing me inside to get warm increases my longing to go home. Even though my illness would return, and Cole and Rose or any of these nice people would end up just being memories, this is a comforting thought. Perhaps Janna is still hanging on and we could visit one last time. I sit down on the grass next to the pond and watch the gentle ripples. Water bugs skim across the surface and that makes me smile.

I love animals and have an appreciation for anything with a heartbeat. Hours have been spent sitting behind my house watching ants march to and fro, and bees collecting pollen from flowers. I even watch worms dig their way into the soil. When it rained, I would pick up worms drowning on the driveway and gently toss them into the garden, until my aunt objected because of my weak immune system. After that, she promised to pick up any stranded worms drowning in a rainfall. Aunt Ruth didn't understand why I cared but she did it anyway because it was important to me. I've never wanted to see her more than right now.

Ebby and Jon tease me about my fascination with bugs because they don't see what I see. When they look at a worm, all they see is a blind, slimy creature that will soon be a bird's lunch. I see a living creature. Yes, worms are blind and there probably isn't much going on in their tiny heads, but this life is all they have. When a worm is squirming in a puddle on the concrete, I see something suffering and want to help. Whatever it is, person, dog, or insect, its life is *all* it has and all it ever will have. That makes it significant. Isn't that a good reason to treat these creatures well for the few days or weeks they have on this earth?

A butterfly darts across the pond, fluttering its wings gently before settling on a lily pad. I study the lawn around me and see an ant marching past. There is a spider perched on a weed growing out of the grass next to me.

The spider is beige, has a larger than normal head and thick legs. A shriek escapes my lips at what I see on closer inspection. This isn't an ordinary spider at all. Its body is spiderlike but its four upper legs look like human arms with hands. Its four lower legs look like human legs with feet. Then there's its face—its teensy face is that of a little boy whose jaw is dropped wide in shock at seeing me. Probably just as much as mine is at seeing him.

Chapter 13

Into the Fog

I LOVE ANIMALS BUT THIS...creature...sends shivers down my spine. It's so unlike anything I've ever seen. The way his human limbs are bent like an insect's is eerie, not to mention the tiny face of a little boy on its human flesh-like, bug-shaped body.

He's definitely more afraid of me than I am of him. Can't blame him though, with me towering over him like a giant. I swear that a tiny screech escapes his mouth but the sound is so faint I can't be certain.

He has a human mouth. Maybe he can talk. Shock has given way to curiosity and I inch my head closer. He steps back, even more frightened.

"It's okay. I won't hurt you. My name is Syn. Do you understand? Can you talk?"

The little critter stares directly into my eyes for a few seconds before he leaps onto a taller blade of grass. He crawls up the blade and lowers himself to the ground on a strand of his web. It's tempting to lift the web in my hand and hold up the spider-boy to try and communicate, but he's too small. There is no guarantee I won't accidently hurt him. He scurries away, hopping across the lawn next to the pond. The way his humanlike limbs move reminds me of those old *Sinbad* and *Jason and the Argonauts* movies on late-night TV, only a tad more fluid than those cheesy, outdated stop-motion effects.

I back away from the pond and keeping my eyes on the spider-boy, follow him alongside the pond from enough distance away to avoid accidently treading on him. Then he stops, looks around like a responsible kid would before crossing the street, and moves westward, away from the pond. Quite curious to see whether there are more creatures like him where he is headed, I continue my pursuit. After seeing the spider-boy and those reptilian dogs that attacked me outside the house, it seems there might be more fantastical creatures living in this Garden.

The spider-boy is in the middle of the lawn between the pond and a cabin when I hear the voices of children nearby. Flint is kicking a ball with two other kids his age—a boy with dark skin and short hair and a girl with blonde hair pulled into a ponytail. The ball and the kids are approaching the area where the spider-boy is crawling.

I dash around the spider-boy and stand in front of the kids. As the ball bounces my way, I scoop it up and hold my arms out to stop them from coming any closer.

"What the heck?" the boy says.

"Are you the new girl?" the girl asks.

"This is Syn," Flint says. "She's the girl I told you about."

"Is something wrong?" the boy asks.

I turn around and scan the grass, panicked. The spider-boy has disappeared, but I know he's there somewhere. "There's this creature…like a spider…and a boy. Don't step on him."

The two kids are startled. Their eyes dart from my face to the grass behind me.

"I'm not making this up. I know what I saw."

"We believe you," Flint says.

"We should tell an adult," the boy says. "Or, I can just squash it."

"No," Flint says. He clenches his hands into small fists. "Please don't. I'll take him back where he belongs."

"But if *she* finds out…" the girl whispers.

"She won't if we don't tell," Flint says. "Don't tell anyone. Either of you. Please."

The two nod at each other, then retreat in the direction they came from.

Flint starts carefully patting the grass around me, searching for the creature. I can see where it is but am not ready to let Flint know.

"You're not going to hurt him, are you?" I ask.

Flint's feelings have been hurt. "Of course not."

Our eyes meet in extended silence.

"I could never do that," he adds.

Finally, I point to the creature. Flint bends down, cups his hands together and scoops up the spider-boy, who frantically scurries across one palm. Flint slides him from hand to hand so he can't escape.

"Hey there," Flint says. "I won't hurt you. I promise."

The creature stops trying to escape and quivers in Flint's hands.

"You hang on and I'll get you home," Flint explains. "Trust me."

I swear there is relief on the spider-boy's face. Did he understand? Or was he comforted by Flint's calming voice? How does Flint know where to take him?

"What is he?" I ask.

"He's a—" Flint interrupts himself. "I have to take him home now." He starts to walk away, keeping his eyes on the creature. Then he turns around and looks at me with a sorrowful expression.

"You can't follow. I'm sorry."

"Why?"

"I'll talk to you later. Just don't tell anyone about this, okay?"

I nod and watch until he's out of sight. This is baffling. Are there actually people here who would want to hurt that little thing? Maybe there are more of these spider-people and they eat the crops or something. It is comforting that Flint cares enough to put him somewhere safe.

I circle around the pond and head to Rose's cabin, feeling quite hungry. Hopefully Rose has an apple or something for me to eat. As I approach the cabin, the front door opens and a girl walks out. The same girl who saved me from the dogs last night.

She looks around suspiciously. When she spots me I wave. She is startled and bolts. Why? Maybe she was trespassing on Rose's property. Nonetheless, in the daylight I see how much she really looks just like me at that age. She was out late when everyone was sleeping, and saved me from being mauled. I not only want to thank her but bet she could answer some of my questions about the house, the woman inside, and probably this entire crazy place.

I lose her as she runs into a stand of trees, heading in the direction of the Square. When I arrive there are eight people, including Rose, chatting and exchanging goods. There's no sign of the girl.

Rose opens her mouth to speak.

"Was there a girl here a minute ago?" I interrupt. "She was running."

Rose is puzzled. "No one here except us."

She was running in this direction. How could no one else have seen her? Then my eyes lock on to some movement about ten feet behind the well. I sprint in that direction and skid to a stop as my path approaches the wall of fog. Standing about ten feet in front of me, directly in front of the fog, is the girl. She glances at me then turns to face the wall of mist and walks right through, disappearing from sight! I run over to where she was and can't see a thing beyond the fog.

Despite Cole's warnings, it's tempting to chase after her. I must talk to this girl, but what if entering the fog causes my CF symptoms to return like climbing the staircase did? Maybe I could go into the fog and turn around if something goes wrong.

I decide to go for it. Gulping the invigorating, moist air, I walk into the thick, gray mist and am immediately enshrouded.

Chapter 14

Crash Landing

IT'S ONLY POSSIBLE TO SEE a few feet ahead when walking through the thick fog. I spin around. I'm barely inside and all I can see is a wall of grayness.

Before going too far, I need to know whether my health is affected. I inhale, exhale, then repeat. The only difference is the moisture and the cooler air. In fact, it feels rather refreshing, like when I let the humidifier breathe on my cheeks as a kid. I cough a few times to make sure phlegm isn't building up in my lungs. I feel fine. Great, in fact.

Relieved, I move on. Besides feeling as healthy as ever, it doesn't seem like this place is alive. Ebby made me sit through this haunted house movie called *Insidious* a couple of years ago, where there was this other dark dimension populated only by the dead. Here, it feels like a dimension outside of my world and the Garden I just came from.

I force myself to stop thinking and focus on finding the girl. I nearly slam into a tree. Except for what's right in front of me, it's hard to see

103

anything. The only way to find the girl is to call out and hope she'll answer.

"Hello?" I pause. "Are you there?" Nothing. "I'd like to talk to you!" Silence. "You saved me from those...dog things last night. I want to thank you!" I wait ten seconds, then ten more. Nothing.

One more step and I bump into a tree. Okay, I better hold my arms out in front like a zombie in those old black and white horror movies (Ebby forced me to watch a couple of those too). I come across more trees. It seems this is a forest. Moss and ferns are growing out of the soil. I hope I'm walking in a straight direction so I can find my way back.

"Hello!" Nothing. "Can you hear me?" Again, nothing. I give up hope of finding the girl here. She must be far ahead by now and who knows how far these woods go.

Going back would be smart, but my curiosity has been piqued. The people in the Garden have given me the impression that the fog is a terrifying place. All I see here are trees and plants. Sure, it's spooky but compared to some of the things in the Garden this is nothing. Plus, Rose told me that the Garden's residents get their supplies in the fog. If I walk far enough, will I end up at a supermarket?

White light flashes in the distance. It disappears, flashes again, and then it's gone. And again. The fourth time the light appears it holds steady for about twenty seconds before disappearing for good. From the corner of my eye, I catch another light flashing far away to my left. It too disappears. This is interesting. When I stood on the balcony at the top of the spiral staircase and looked down at the fog below, there were lights flashing. From up there the fog seemed to go on forever. Like there was no end or exit.

As baffling as this is, it's not all that scary. It's intriguing. Before continuing though, I make note of the direction of my path so that finding my way back will be easy. After a few minutes of trekking through the foggy forest, there have only been trees, stumps, and small plants to see. I trip over something. Excited that this might be something interesting, I bend down, peering through the mist curiously. It's just a large rock.

There is no sign of any wildlife. Walking in the woods as a kid, there had never been any bears to see, but there was always the odd deer, lots of birds and squirrels, and the sound of creatures rustling in the bushes. Here, it's utterly silent. Even when alone at home in my bedroom there are occasional creaks as the house shifts, and humming from the heater or the refrigerator. Here, the only sound is from my footsteps and breathing. It's rather peaceful but why aren't there animals in this forest? Or insects? Is there something terrifying here that I haven't come across yet? Still, the thought doesn't dissuade me from venturing on, because it's so pleasant out here.

There is another flash in the distance. Again, two flashes and then one that glows steadily for about twenty seconds. Then there's another flash to my far left. Something about these flashes seems familiar. But what?

I creep ahead for a while before tripping again, this time falling flat on the dirt. My hands and knees are scraped. In this place, these scrapes are bound to heal in no time. I get up, a bit sore but all right. I'm going to have to use Rose's shower later. Or maybe take a bath. The thought of soothing, soapy water on my body makes me smile, even though my hands and knees are stinging.

I look down, expecting to see another rock. Instead, there is a narrow chunk of metal at my feet. It's painted white and is about my height in length and my forearm in width. It's scratched and dirty and its jagged edges tell me it's likely a piece of something that broke off of another object. There is something to my right, obscured by the fog. A couple of steps closer and something big comes into view. I bend down to touch it— another piece of metal—and trail my fingers along its length, trying to feel where it goes. This is huge. While walking around the object, realization of what it is hits and let out a shriek.

This is a small airplane. Part of the wing is missing. The piece of metal I tripped over earlier might be the missing part. Aside from a couple people in the cockpit, the plane wouldn't carry more than eight passengers. Its door is ajar.

Panic sets in. Do the people in the Garden know about this? How long has it been here? Is it empty or filled with dead passengers? When I was on top of the staircase a plane flew over the endless fog. Is this place full of planes that crashed? Maybe this is why everyone's terrified of this place. Because it's full of dead people.

I could be overreacting. This one airplane doesn't mean there are more in the forest. It has obviously been here a while so there won't be anyone to save. No good can come of it, but I can't just walk away without checking. I poke my head inside. There is just enough light to see that the passenger seats are empty. I sigh with relief.

Debris and dirt are scattered throughout the dusty interior. Several seatbelts and their buckles are strewn across the floor. The only item within reach without climbing into the plane—I have no intention of doing that!—is a yellow sheet of paper lying on the floor. I touch a toe to an edge and slide it over to me. It's a carbon copy of the flight manifest. It's damp and too faded to read in detail here so I fold it up and put it in my pocket.

At the front of the plane, windows are broken and shattered glass litters the ground. There are no bodies in the cockpit either. Another huge sigh of relief escapes me. Once on a field trip to a wooded national park, some boys said they were hoping to come across skeletons. I didn't understand why anyone would wish for that.

There's another flash of light in the distance and then one to my left that's much farther away. Again, to the left, another flash and then another and one that holds steady. What is it about these flashes that is so familiar? It's sort of like watching lightning. But that's not it.

Then it hits me! When I fell into my pond there was a white light in the water right before I blacked out. That white light was similar to the flashes at the end of the sequence—the ones that hold steady for a short time.

If my arrival in this world was through one of these flashes, could one of them also take me home? Rose's first thought was that I came here through the fog. Could the scary aspects in the fog actually be part of my own world? Do these people enter the fog and travel through the light into my world, buy supplies and then head back? That wouldn't be too terrifying for me—it's just home. But for these people, who live in a world without much technology that might be scary. I mean, they probably have never seen a car before or even flashing lights at an intersection.

As much as I like Rose, Flint, Cole and the others, as much as there are countless questions that need answers, and as much as I enjoy being healthy, as Dorothy Gale said in *The Wizard of Oz*, "There's no place like home." My aunt is surely worried sick. The police will be searching for me. And maybe, just maybe, Janna is still alive.

That light might take me home or nowhere at all, or someplace else. But I have to try! As soon as the next series of flashes begins, I take a deep breath, hold my arms out in front, and sprint toward the flashing light.

Chapter 15

The Light

BEFORE I CAN REACH THE light, another light flashes. Just like the others, there are three quick flashes and then the light holds for a number of seconds before blinking out. Could each light be a gateway to other places? Which one will take me home, if any?

There is something massive lying on the ground. I go to check it out and can't believe my eyes. Another crashed airplane!

The cockpit has been ground a few feet into the dirt. There are at least five toppled trees nearby, likely felled by the crash. I place a hand on the surface of the cockpit and slide it along, while walking the length of the aircraft. As damp dirt rubs off on my fingers, I realize this isn't a small plane like the other one. There are dozens of broken windows and the wing is gigantic, looming through the mist. I'm standing next to a jet airliner.

I shiver at the thought of all the bodies that could be rotting inside. But there isn't any smell and there weren't any in the smaller plane so there probably aren't any in this one either. Perhaps the residents of the Garden removed the bodies? Or maybe the Garden's residents are survivors of this flight? Regardless, the plane has obviously been here a long time. Just the thought of hundreds of dead bodies possibly being inside the plane at some point in time freaks me out. I don't even want to think about it.

I also try not to think about the likelihood that there are more downed planes in this fog. It seems that the fog surrounding the Garden stretches for a great distance. I've only walked through a small portion of it and have already come across two aircraft. There must be some reason why they crashed here. A chill runs down my spine. This discovery gives me one more reason to go home.

The light flashes again in the same direction I had just been running. I circle around the airliner, raise my arms and head to the light. I'm just a few minutes away when the feeling that I'm not alone returns. Is that girl nearby? Or someone else? I stop and listen. There is only silence. Maybe I was mistaken. This is not the first time I've felt like I was being watched though. I keep going.

A few minutes later more light flashes to my left and then in front of me. Once. Twice. A third time. In twenty paces I can walk into the long, fourth flash. Let's do this.

As I start to take one of what may be my last steps in this strange land, a hand grips my shoulder. I turn around in a panic and see a woman with a hood pulled over her face. She lowers the hood.

"Rose! What are you doing here?"

"Stopping you from making a terrible mistake."

"I have to go home!"

"Walking through that light isn't going to take you there. It will take you someplace else. Someplace that isn't safe."

A lump forms in my throat and cold tears stream down my cheeks. "I have to do this. I *need* to go home where I belong."

"I know. But this isn't going to take you there."

"How do you know? Have you walked through the light?"

Rose lowers her eyes. "No." She raises her gaze to mine again, holding back tears of her own. "My husband did. He never came home."

"Oh."

"Only a few people in the Garden are designated to come out here for supplies—all men. My husband was one of them. Every time he went into the light he ended up someplace new. Sometimes he was able to get food and supplies from a peaceful place. Other times the horror was so great he wouldn't even speak of it. About three years ago he went out for supplies and never returned."

Rose doesn't hold back the tears anymore. I look into her sad eyes and embrace her in my arms.

"I'm so sorry."

She pulls away. "It's possible you may end up somewhere nice. But you may end up somewhere awful. Each time the light flashes it will take you someplace new. Roy never went to the same place twice. So, you can't count on it taking you home."

My tears continue to flow. "I can't stay here forever! I have no idea where I am! And I've seen things that scare me." I point behind us. "I've already found two crashed planes! What are they doing here? Why are the woods covered in fog? Why are there flashing lights that take you to random places? I'm so confused and lost here."

"Come back with me. Cole is gathering everyone who lives in the Garden. We're going to put our heads together and find a way to get you home. We'll help you. I promise."

I try to regain my composure, fully aware that it would be a huge gamble to walk through that light. Cole and the others should have a chance to help before I do something rash. I nod, and Rose leads me back to the Garden, her arm around my shoulder.

We walk in silence until we reach the jet airliner. I pull away from Rose. "Do you know what happened here? Are there more?"

Rose studies the airliner for a moment, then puts her arm around my shoulder again. "I don't have all the answers. But let me tell you what I know."

Chapter 16

The Day the Sky Fell Down

ROSE AND I CAREFULLY WALK through the fog. I'm excited yet anxious to maybe get some answers about this strange place.

"The planes..." Rose trails off and we both stop walking. She looks straight into my eyes, then sighs and lowers her head. "If I tell you where the planes came from you'll have even more questions. Why don't I start at the beginning?"

I nod, trying not to let my anticipation show.

"When I was about ten years older than you are, I woke up not far from where my cabin is now, with no memories of anything that occurred before that. I understood English and knew some things—like the green groundcover I was sitting on was called grass—but had no idea who I was. Or who my parents were. Or what I did the day before. I even had no clue what my name was."

Through the mist of the fog, Rose's sadness is obvious as she recalls her beginnings in the Garden.

"I stood up and looked around," she continues. "The Garden looked much like it does today, only without the cabins. There were others walking about, just as lost as me. A young man was staring at me from across the pond. I couldn't see him well in the distance yet felt an instantaneous connection with him. Like we had known each other our entire lives. When we came face to face, we gazed into each other's eyes, mesmerized. Then we embraced. Even though no memories resurfaced, we knew we belonged together."

"That was your husband?"

Rose smiled. "Yes. That was Roy. We never married. It felt like we had been in another lifetime and that was good enough for us. Anyway, the two of us, along with some of the others, explored our surroundings. The sky was cloudy at this time, though the Garden was warm and humid. We were entranced by the spiral staircase. It seemed like it was plucked out of a mansion—which was a strange thing to think because I had no recollection of ever being inside a mansion or a house of any kind. And the cloud that hovered near the top. There are no words. You've seen it?"

I nod.

"Roy went to the bottom of the stairs and was about to climb the first step when the sky abruptly darkened. The clouds grew heavier and we felt rain for the first time since awakening in the Garden. It was torrential. We huddled under the staircase and still got soaked from water dripping off each step. A bird fell out of the sky and bounced off one of the steps. More birds hit the grass farther away. The one near us was convulsing. It was horrible to watch. Then we heard roaring in the sky that sounded like a plane. We crept from under the staircase and looked up. It was impossible to see anything through the thick clouds. The plane was heading north by the sound of it. More birds had fallen to the ground. They appeared to be dead but we ran past them so fast it's hard to say for sure.

"While we were in the orchard there was a powerful boom. I can't describe how loud it was. It should have shaken the ground but it didn't. Several others were running into the fog to see what happened. We followed. As soon as we entered the fog there was no more rain. Nothing was wet and even the sound of rain had stopped.

"Flames were glowing in the distance. It was a long walk through the fog until we reached the plane. Even though there were fires burning, Roy and a few of the others searched for survivors. As they tried to pry open the door we heard another roar. It turned out to be a helicopter that had crashed and exploded."

"Oh my god."

"There was no god here. Only carnage and mayhem. I went with a few others to investigate the second crash. When we arrived the wreck was partly dug into the earth and there was more smoke than fire from the explosion. The door of the helicopter was open and the pilot and passenger were dead."

"They died? Why didn't the Garden heal them?"

"If there was even a trace of life left before they hit the ground that would have been possible. They were dead on impact. We left the fog shaken up and saddened, but everything was different. Once we left the fog, it was cold and snow was falling. It was too cold to stay out there for long so we returned to the fog. Shortly thereafter, we heard another crash at the opposite end of the Garden. And then another. And another. And the weather kept changing. From snow, to rain, to intense heat, to what it is like today. For reasons I will never understand, each time the weather changed, planes and helicopters fell out of the sky and crashed into the fog. A few hours later, the weather had leveled out at a warm temperature with a mostly clear sky. Any changes in weather after that were normal. And once the abrupt changes in the sky had stopped, so had the rain of death from above. The birds that had fallen were gone. Maybe the Garden's healing elements helped them? But the planes… From what we had found, we guessed over twenty aircraft crashed that day. There were no survivors."

Rose bites her lip.

"Do you know what happened? What caused the sky to change and the planes to fall?"

She shakes her head. "We have no idea. Following that horrible day, we gradually started to get things in order. After a few weeks of eating only fruits and vegetables, some of the men ventured into the fog to see how far it went, and to search for supplies. They walked through the light and ended up in another place. We got saws, cut down trees, and used them to build cabins. Some of us knew exactly how to build things or do plumbing, like it had been our job in a previous lifetime. Over time, we became a pleasant society. It was peaceful. Roy and I eventually had Flint."

Rose smiles and starts to walk again.

I wait at least another minute before asking my next question. "Are the bodies from the planes buried in the cemetery outside of the big house?"

Maybe it's the fog but Rose's face seems to turn white. After a moment she answers.

"No. We buried them in a mound on the east side of the fog. I don't know who's buried outside the house. Nobody knows. It's one of those questions most of us would rather not know the answer to."

I don't say anything for a few minutes. Rose stops and faces me.

"Things have been pretty good here. But even after we got settled we had our fair share of tragedy too. Too many of our men have been lost to wherever the fog took them."

She puts both hands on my shoulders. "Syn, I know you want to go home. We're going to try and make that happen. Please understand that leaving through the fog won't get you there. I need you to promise that you won't try to go out there again."

There is much pain in Rose's eyes and her grip on my shoulders is intense. I can't help but nod. Her hands loosen and she pulls me into a hug.

When we reach the border of the fog, Rose stops again. "Please keep this conversation to yourself. Don't speak about what we talked about, not even to me."

"Why not?"

"The woman in the house. She sees everything in the Garden. And she leaves us alone as long as we live our own lives and keep to ourselves. But she wouldn't take it lightly if one of us shared our history with an outsider. She can't see or hear what happens in the fog but in the Garden, nothing gets past her."

I'm about to ask Rose more about the woman but she walks straight ahead and disappears. I sigh and follow her to the Garden. She prepares meatloaf with rice and beans for dinner. I'm not proud that I eat animals (my doctors insist) but can't deny that this meatloaf is delicious. Since I haven't seen any cows or rice fields here, I'm guessing this food was sourced from the fog—from whatever exists through the flashes of light.

After dinner, I take a long bath, soaking in the tub for more than an hour. Rose knocks on the bathroom door twice to make sure everything is okay. The day's events gradually clear from my mind and blessed relaxation sets in.

Once I'm out of the tub and all dried off, Rose tells me that Cole came by. The gathering is a go and he'll see me tomorrow. Again, I play a game of Battleship with Rose and Flint (Flint wins again.). The game is boring but I really enjoy spending time with the two of them.

Flint turns off his light first. I lie there with my light on thinking about all those crashed planes. All those people who died. Where did they come from? Are they from my world? Another world? Were they in this world before everyone here woke up with no memories? And if they aren't buried in the cemetery outside the house, who *is* buried there?

Frustrated about having more questions than answers, I reach out to turn off my light, and remember the flight manifest stuffed into my jeans pocket. I get up and tiptoe over to my jeans, which are folded on a chair by the window, and retrieve the crumpled piece of paper. Settling back into bed, I unfold it and start reading.

The plane was privately owned by Jasper Inc. and the manifest is dated March 24, 2001. That was a couple of years before my parents disappeared. I was three years old. There is a short list of names: the pilot—James Rogan—and four passengers: Jesse Jasper, Jessica Mayfield, Bobby Ness, and Mark Wu.

I recognize two of the names. Jesse Jasper is a famous billionaire, heir to his parents' real estate empire. Unlike so many kids who grow up with money handed to them, Jesse is well-known for donating more than half of his wealth to important causes and raising awareness about environmental issues such as protecting the rainforests and saving endangered species. He's an adrenaline junkie and likes the party life, but he's well-respected for all the good work he has done with his fortune.

There are two notable things about seeing Jesse Jasper's name on the manifest. First, he's from my world. Second, and most importantly, he is very much alive and well! He certainly didn't die in 2001. He was on TV not long ago promoting a documentary he narrated about global warming and its effect on the rising ocean levels. This name on the manifest could be someone else named Jesse Jasper, except the next name in the manifest indicates otherwise.

Jessica Mayfield was a young actress who died a few years ago from a drug overdose. Not in 2001 and certainly not in a plane crash. Plus, she dated Jesse Jasper when they were in their early twenties. It has to be them—this can't be a coincidence.

Chapter 17

The Gathering

I DON'T REMEMBER EXACTLY WHAT my dream was about, just that when my eyes open there is an image of Janna. Not from the last time I saw her, pale and weak. It was Janna at her best, offering an exceptionally glowing smile with perfectly straight white teeth that would erase anybody's sadness.

The thought of her saddens me. It's been three days since paying a visit to her and I don't know if she's still alive. She could be lying in her hospital bed right now preparing to fade away or she could have passed the very day of our last visit. I don't delude myself into thinking she could be on a surprise road to recovery, but the only thing worse than not knowing is the very real chance that I'll *never* know.

I *need* to go home.

Rose serves me a toasted English muffin for breakfast and sets a bowl of fruit in the center of the table. "Don't eat too much because there will be lots of food at the gathering Cole is putting together."

"It's really happening!"

Rose returns my glowing smile. "Later this morning at 11:30."

After breakfast, I take a quick shower. Flint is in Rose's room pulling his shirt on as I leave the washroom, the scales on his back in plain view. When he turns around he simply grins at me. Flint knows he can trust me and that makes me happy. Hopefully I can visit this place and see these wonderful people after returning home.

Wonderful people. Those two words would never be used by me to describe anyone at home other than Janna. Even with all the uncertainty, I am happier here than at home. Still, I need to go home to set my aunt's mind at ease and make peace with Janna's fate.

It's just after ten so I decide to go for a walk before Cole's gathering. Maybe sit under a tree or by the pond. Enjoy my time in this beautiful place before leaving.

Lily is at the pond, sitting at the edge dangling her feet in the water. She doesn't hear me approach. I consider leaving her alone to enjoy the moment, then change my mind and decide to say hello.

"Hi there," Lily says, turning her head. She pats the spot on the grass next to her. "Do you want to join me?"

Her offer seems sincere so I sit cross-legged beside her.

Lily laughs. "I hate that you look better in my clothes than I do."

Lily is a sweet girl. Back at home, a pretty girl like her would avoid eye contact with me in the hallway and treat Ebby like crap. Lily wouldn't do that. She seems genuinely nice. "Thanks again for loaning me the clothes. I'd feel gross wearing the same thing every day."

"No worries. The water is perfect. You should dip your feet in."

I put my hand in the water and it's warm. Warmer than it would be in my pond at this time of year. I slide off my sandals and dip my feet into the water. It feels good. I lower my calves in.

"See?"

I smile. After a few minutes of enjoying the gentle breeze and Lily's company, I lie back on the ground. Lily follows my lead and we lie there in silence, occasionally looking each other's way and sharing brief, polite conversation. Eventually, Lily's eyes close and I'm pretty sure she's asleep, or close to it.

I lie there for some time, staring up at the clear sky. Very few moments in my life have been as perfect as this. Yet when a couple walks by carrying blankets and picnic baskets excitement about the gathering churns inside.

"How long were we out?" Lily is yawning herself awake.

"A while. I don't have the time."

She sits up and pulls an old silver timepiece from her shorts pocket. "It's close to 11:30. We should get going. You don't want to miss your own celebration."

"Celebration? What are we celebrating? This is supposed to be a brainstorming session to get me home."

Lily just hugs me. "I'll see you at the Square soon."

On my way back to the cabin, more people pass who are probably heading to the Square. They wave hello. Rose is just coming through the doorway of her cabin when I arrive.

"Oh, good. I was going to go find you. Wait here." She slips inside and returns with Flint and a blanket.

As the three of us approach the Square, the chatter gets louder.

There are at least two dozen gathered in the Square, many of whom I haven't seen yet. Kids are running around playing. There is a buffet— pastries, fruit, and beverages—and a few are already holding a plate or a cup. Some look my way and smile but most of them haven't noticed me yet.

Standing by the well talking to Nell and a man who looks about fifty, is Cole. He glances my way, smiles, and starts winding his way through the crowd. Nell and the other man follow.

Cole gives me a hug. "Told you I'd get everyone together, didn't I?"

"You did."

"It's good to see you again, Syn," Nell says. She tilts her head toward the man next to her. "This is my dad, Hopper. Dad, this is Syn."

Hopper reaches out and gently shakes my hand. "It's a pleasure to meet you, young lady."

Many eyes are focused in my direction now. Faces are smiling like they know me. Wolf is on the other side of the Square. When he sees me, he jumps up and down, higher than a man that age should be able to, and waves.

Cole takes my hand. "Hey everyone," he says, projecting his voice. "Thanks for coming today. I'd like to introduce Syn, who is new to the Garden and who we have gathered here today to meet."

Everyone applauds. I force a smile, uncomfortable with Cole introducing me like I'm a new resident.

"Syn came to the Garden a few days ago and has been staying with Rose and Flint. If you haven't met her yet, please introduce yourselves."

Cole lets go of my hand and pats my back as people start to line up like guests do at a wedding to congratulate the bride and groom. He leaves me to the greeters and walks over to the well with Lily and Fern while a flurry of voices bombard me.

"How happy we are to see a new face here."

"Please stop by if you ever need anything."

What about finding me a way home?

Wolf gives me a hug. "How are you doing, young lady?"

"I'm okay." I realize my forced smile has worn off. "This is nice but Cole told me that people were gathering to help find a way to get me home."

"There's plenty of time for that. Now is the time to meet new friends and enjoy good food. I picked the apples in that apple pie myself."

"Excuse me." I walk out of the Square.

Cole lied to me. He was hoping this party would show me how welcoming everyone is and convince me to stay. Either he doesn't believe there's a way for me to go home or he would rather I stay here. That's *not* an option!

Cole may have given up but I haven't. Aside from going into the light in the fog, which Rose says won't get me home, there's one other possibility. I head for the pond.

Soon I'm standing at the spot that resembles where I was sitting at home when I fell in. I make sure no one has followed me and take off my top, leaving my bra on. I toss the shirt to the grass and cautiously look around once more, then off come my sandals and shorts. Wearing nothing but underwear has me feeling extremely vulnerable.

I sit down on the grass and dip my legs into the warm water, hesitating. Only knowing how to dog paddle could be a problem. The water in the pond at home isn't too deep though, so as long as it's not much deeper here it should be okay. I check behind me one more time, close my eyes, and slide into the water.

Chapter 18

Blast from the Past

AFTER BEING UNDERWATER FOR MERE seconds, I start to freak out. I paddle my arms, pull my head above the water and hold tightly to the edge, hoping the commotion didn't attract any attention.

Not good. I let go of the edge with one hand, wipe the water from my eyes, and push the wet hair off my face. After filling my lungs with air, I push myself back under the water, keeping my eyes closed. I know my destination. I pivot my body so my head points toward the bottom of the pond and kick my feet. After a few seconds, my hand feels a large rock and my eyes fly open. There is no light. Nothing flashing, nothing bright. Just mud, stones covered in algae, and a few small fish. I spin, stretch out my arms and kick my feet until the grassy edge is within reach.

I stay in the water for a moment, letting the water lap at the bottom of my chin and then pull myself up. Dropping down on the grass, a sense of failure washes over me. I pull my knees to my chest, wrap my arms around them, and allow the tears to flow.

"Syn?"

I spin around on the grass, keeping my knees against my chest so Cole can't see through my wet bra. He and Lily are standing a few feet away with concern on their faces.

"What's wrong?" Cole asks. "We were looking for you." He comes closer and I flinch.

Lily touches his elbow. "Go get Syn a towel."

"Yeah. Of course."

Cole runs off and Lily drops to her knees and wraps her arms around me.

"You're going to get all wet."

"I don't care," she responds. "Do you want to talk about it?"

Her genuine concern is so touching I burst into tears. As the tears are subsiding, Cole is standing a few feet away holding a towel, an awkward expression on his face. Lily grabs the towel and wraps it around me. I use the top edge to wipe the remaining tears from my face.

"Are you okay, Syn?" Cole asks. "What happened?"

"I went looking for the light I saw when I fell into my pond at home."

"Oh, Syn," Cole says. "I did the same thing the day after you arrived. There was no light down there."

"You did? Why didn't you tell me?"

"Thought I did. Why are you doing this? Everyone in the Garden has come to meet you. You're the guest of honor."

"Guest of honor! You said it was a brainstorming session. To find a way for me to go home. It wasn't like that at all. Everyone was buttering me up, trying to make me feel at home. Trying to make me want to stay."

Cole sighs. "Okay, you're partly right. We don't want you to leave. I also respect that you want to go home. An hour before the gathering started I met with eight of the smartest people here at the Square. There was no reason to involve everyone. Yes, the gathering was to welcome you. But I promise, we really tried to think of a way to get you home before everyone else arrived."

"Did you figure out a way?"

"To be honest, we didn't come up with much. There are a few things to consider, nothing concrete. But don't give up hope."

Hopelessness envelops me. No more tears come. There is just numbness.

Lily places her hand on my shoulder. "We'll leave you to get dressed."

"Please stop by the Square again, even if you don't stay long," says Cole, glancing at Lily.

"Yes, just come say hello and then we can leave together."

I'm ticked at Cole, but because Lily is being so kind I reluctantly nod in agreement. She hugs me again and then they walk away.

I dry off and after making sure no one is watching, take off my underwear and pull my shorts and T-shirt on. I don't like how it feels to go commando so I stop at Rose's and put on a fresh pair of underpants.

When I return to the Square, most of the people are still there. Cole approaches me eagerly.

"Can I get you anything?"

I shake my head and walk away, not wanting him to forget I'm mad at him for misleading me.

"Here you go, young lady." Wolf intercepts my path, grinning, and hands me a paper plate heaping full of his apple pie. "Enjoy."

A little farther along, as I'm lifting a forkful of pie to my mouth, Flint tugs on my other wrist. "Where did you go?"

"It doesn't matter. I'm back now."

I walk on, feeling quite down, not wanting to talk to anyone. *I've got to get out of here.* Before leaving, I spot a face I recognize.

Wolf is talking to a fifty-something man with a trimmed white beard and mustache—Joel Anderson, a neighbor of mine from back home! He and his wife Maggie run an exotic animal refuge about a block from my house. When I was a kid, I walked down to his place almost every week and he or Maggie would show me the latest creatures that had been rescued or dropped off. Last year he asked me to volunteer during the summer. Aunt Ruth convinced me that it was too risky because of my health issues. She was probably right.

"You're back!" Lily says. "Listen, I—"

"I need to see someone." Brushing past my new friend, I march over to Mr. Anderson and Wolf.

Wolf flashes me his uncannily white smile. "Well, hello again, darling. How does the pie taste?"

"Hi, Wolf. Mr. Anderson?"

He looks at me blankly, as if he doesn't even realize I'm talking to him.

"Mr. Anderson?" I repeat. "Don't you recognize me?"

"Syn, this is Docson," Wolf says.

The man—Docson—extends his hand. "Nice to meet you, Syn."

"You're not Joel Anderson?"

"Me?" Docson asks in surprise. "No, never heard that name before."

"What about Maggie? Maggie Anderson."

Docson shakes his head. "No, there's no one named Maggie in the Garden."

Lily, Wolf, and Docson are all wearing puzzled expressions.

"It's good to meet you," I say and quickly walk away.

Lily catches up. "What's going on, Syn? Are you all right?"

"No, I'm not all right!" I throw my plate of pie to the ground. "That man—Docson—is someone I know from home. His real name is Joel Anderson!"

Lily jumps, caught off guard by my rising temper. "I'm confused."

"*You're* confused? How about me? I fell into a pond at home—no, I was *pushed* in—and woke up here. This place—this *Garden* is like an alternate version of home except that here no one gets sick. And, there's a masked woman living in the house I grew up in, creatures that shouldn't even exist, a staircase that takes you right up into the sky, fog with light portals that take you who knows where and *you're* confused?!"

"I'm sorry, Syn. Really. But I'm your friend, and would help you get home if there was a way. Honest!"

Lily is hurt.

"Forgive me. You've been so nice. Everything just makes me feel so...helpless. I need to leave this place. I just have to! Even if walking into a flash of light takes me somewhere random, at least I tried *something!*"

"Syn," Cole says from behind me.

I turn around. "What do *you* want?"

Cole places his hand on Lily's shoulder. "Can you excuse us for a minute?"

It's obvious Lily doesn't feel comfortable leaving.

"I need to talk to Syn," Cole insists. "Alone."

I nod to Lily. "It's okay. I'll see you later. Sorry for yelling at you."

"There's nothing to be sorry about. Come by for dinner, okay?" She glances over at Cole and then at me. "You too, Cole."

Once she's gone, Cole takes my right hand in both of his. "I know you're feeling lost," he whispers. "You're scared and want answers." He glances around us, then gently pulls me to the back of the Garden.

"Cole—"

"Hush."

Cole leads me toward the fog and then into it.

Chapter 19

The House

"I HOPE YOU'RE NOT scared," Cole says, no longer whispering.

"I'm not." I realize he thinks this place is new to me and decide not to tell him otherwise. "What's going on? You told me it's not safe to come in here."

"Not alone, no. And certainly not too far. It's just..." Cole stares at the ground, trying to find his words. "If you want to have a conversation away from prying ears, this is the best place."

"But if there was someone listening you couldn't see them anyway."

Cole looks around, habitually worried that someone could be listening in the fog, although he can't see through it any better than I can. "You never know who's listening when you're in the Garden," he says.

"You're talking about that woman in the house, aren't you?" I remembered Rose telling me that she couldn't hear or see anything in the fog.

"You want answers, I understand. I'll tell you everything. In a minute."

Cole takes my hand and leads me farther. Eventually, we come to a large stump. Cole certainly knows this place well. He lets go of my hand, motions for me to sit down, and sits next to me.

"Yes, to answer your question," he says. "The person who sees and hears everything in the Garden is the woman in the house. No one knows how she does this."

"Who is she? Is she bad?"

Cole opens his mouth, then shuts it. "You have lots of questions," he says after a moment. "I'll start at the beginning. Before that woman was living in the house."

Before? My ears are perked up with anticipation. "Was she one of the original people who woke up here or is she an outsider like me?"

"The first memories I have," Cole begins, raising a hand to silence my questions, "are from when I was about four, and waking up in the Garden with a few others. None of us could remember who we were. A man and a woman who woke up near me took me under their wing. Together, we explored the Garden."

"No memories at all? You didn't even know your name?"

"No one did. We gave each other names pretty quickly though—it's hard to communicate with people when you have nothing to call them. The man and the woman named themselves Adam and Root. We named ourselves after things found in the Garden. Plants and stones…my name is short for coleus, which is a plant you'll find in the Garden. Strangely, we knew the names of many things even though we couldn't remember our own."

"Coleuses are beautiful. We have them in our garden at home too. Why Adam?"

Cole smirks. "Root gave him that name. She didn't know anything about herself, though she remembered portions of the Bible and named him after the first man."

I nod, excited to hear more.

"So, Adam and Root and I, along with some of the others, explored the Garden. Before long, we found the big house. Gathered in front of it was another group. They weren't all human."

"*Not human?*"

"Right. Only one of them was human. Wolf. Standing with him were four…creatures. We didn't know what to call them at first. Eventually we referred to them as Creepers."

"Creepers?"

"Yeah." He pointed to his face. "You know how I look like two different people merged together? Well, the Creepers didn't look like this. Instead, they looked like their DNA had been merged with an animal's."

An image of Flint's tail and scales swims through my mind, which Rose made me promise not to talk about. The spider-boy is probably a Creeper as well! I open my mouth to tell Cole about the crocodile-dog creatures that attacked me—

"Two of the creatures were like crocodiles who stood upright like we do. Another was covered in brown and white fur. The fourth one looked like a fifty-year-old man except his eyes were narrowed like a cat's. He had a snake-like, forked tongue that slithered in and out of his mouth every few seconds."

A few days ago this would have sounded extremely far-fetched, but after what I've experienced it doesn't surprise me as much as it probably should.

"The guy with the slithering tongue couldn't talk. Wolf and the other three told us they also woke up with no memories. Our two groups joined forces and decided to check out the house to see if anyone lived there. The door was open so Adam and Wolf went inside. After a few minutes they came out and motioned for us to come in, saying no one was inside."

"What was in the house?"

"The main floor was one big room with computer equipment and cardboard boxes stacked up."

I had expected it to look more like my place back home, with the dining room, living room and kitchen on the main floor. I'm still intrigued, though a little disappointed.

"The basement was dusty and seemed like it was mostly used for storage. Lots more boxes down there. There were three bedrooms and two washrooms on the top floor. Two of the bedrooms were unfurnished. One of the washrooms wasn't functional. The master bedroom looked lived in, with a king-size bed and two night tables, each with lamps and books on them. There was soap and shampoo in the attached master bathroom, and drinking glasses and toothbrushes on the counter. One of the sinks was still wet."

He pauses, staring absentmindedly through the fog.

"Well, did you find out who was living there?" I squirm. My butt is already sore from sitting on the hard stump. Mostly though, my curiosity is brimming over.

"Eventually."

Cole picks up a twig and twirls it between his fingers. I can hardly stand the suspense. "Go on."

"We each took turns using the bathroom, got cleaned up and headed back downstairs. Wolf stopped in his tracks at the bottom of the stairs, halting us all behind him.

"'Hello?' he said.

"Standing by the door was a man and a woman, in their mid-thirties and nicely dressed. They seemed nervous but were pleasant. Wolf asked if they had awakened here too. The man told him that they came here some time ago. And that this was their house."

An idea comes to me with a startling shiver. *This* could change everything. Is it possible? Could it be—?

"These people," I barely manage, "who lived in the house. What did they look like?"

Cole seems surprised by the question.

"The man was about my height, the woman a bit shorter. He had a graying, brown beard and hair. That doesn't matter. They—"

"It does matter. Trust me. What did the woman look like?"

"Brown hair also. Now that I think about it, she looked a bit like you."

"Do—" I can barely get my words out. "Do you know their names?"

"Ian and Deb."

My hands grasp at my chest. I can barely breathe.

Cole drops the twig. He touches my arm. "Syn?"

"Those people you saw?"

"Yes?"

"They were my parents."

Chapter 20

A New Hope

My mind flashes back to when I was five, recalling the bristly feeling of my dad's beard on my forehead as he tucked me in and kissed me goodnight; my mom's beautiful, shiny brown hair and how she used to tease my dad about his beard going gray.

Cole raises his eyebrows. "Your *parents*?"

"They disappeared when I was five. This Garden must be where they went."

"Disappeared?"

"They were there one night and gone the next morning. Except for a short time in foster care, I've been living with my aunt ever since."

Cole puts his hand on mine. "I'm sorry. I know how it feels to grow up without parents."

We look at the ground, and then at each other.

"That house," I say. "It's almost identical to the one at home. I don't understand any of this."

His hand tightens over mine.

"But, isn't it possible my parents came here just like me? And they got stuck here too? My parents could still be here somewhere!"

"Oh, Syn." Cole strokes my hand. "Please don't get too excited. I don't think they're here anymore."

I pull my hand free as my heart sinks. "Why not?"

"A lot has happened since that day. The man and woman were very kind. They said we were free to use their facilities so long as we didn't touch their equipment and belongings. In the days, weeks and months to come, our people worked with the Creepers to grow crops and build shelters. Adam and Root took care of me. I helped them on the farm, when able."

"How about my parents? Were they part of your society too?"

"They kept to themselves. In fact, once we had built shelters for ourselves, they closed off the house. After that, they would just come and go."

"Come and go where?"

"I don't know. Sometimes the house was vacant and they were just…gone. Eventually they'd come back."

As a kid, I spent a lot of time with a nanny because my parents were away so often. Who would have believed where they were really going?

"But they're gone now," Cole says.

"Gone?"

"Let me finish," Cole says impatiently. "You have questions and I'm trying to answer them."

I'm desperate to know what happened to my parents. *Got to be patient. Got to trust Cole to get there on his own.*

"You see," Cole continues, "we lived in harmony with the Creepers for several years, and shared resources. We kept to ourselves. The couple in the house...your parents... They were friendly when our paths crossed, although they didn't spend much time in the Garden even when they were home. Mostly, they stayed in the house. I'm not sure why.

"Anyways, while things were fairly peaceful, there were...tragedies. People went out into the fog for supplies and never returned."

"Like Rose's husband," I say quietly.

"Yes, like him. Some were even killed."

"Killed? This doesn't make any sense. I thought everyone in the Garden lived forever."

"No one will die of natural causes. But if someone's heart is cut out, or they fall from up high and break their neck, or if they are...burned so that there's nothing left, there's no way back."

I don't know what to say.

"I'm sorry to tell you these things," Cole says. "Yes, it's disturbing. But you wanted to know."

I nod.

"You remember that staircase I showed you on the other side of the Garden?"

"Of course."

"Some were dragged up there and killed on the platform at the top of the stairs."

A cold shiver ripples up and down my spine. In that spot where I almost died, people were murdered?

"About five or six years ago, I was returning to our cabin and saw smoke. The cabin was on fire. Adam and Root were screaming for help. Three Creepers with blood on their clothes ran out through the front door. I'll never forget the depraved smiles on their faces." Cole clenches his fists and swallows hard. "I tried to save them. Everyone did. But the fire intensified and then the screaming just...stopped. Adam and Root were gone. They were the only parents I've ever known."

"I'm so sorry, Cole."

"Adam and Root's deaths were the last straw. Now we knew the Creepers were the ones killing our family and friends. We joined forces, rounded them all up and banished them from the Garden."

"Were they all involved in the murders?"

"Probably not. We didn't know who was involved and who wasn't. But we didn't care. It wasn't safe with them here and everybody in the Garden agreed to banish them. Except for Ian and Deb. Wolf and I went to the house to talk to them. To let them know about the plan and to ask for help. There was no answer when we knocked on the front door. We tried again. Nothing, that is until we were walking away. The door creaked open.

"Curious, I snuck inside and the door slammed shut behind me. Wolf banged on it for a few seconds. Then there was nothing, except for a low humming sound. It was dark. My eyes strained to adjust to dim lights from the computer equipment and the blue glow from a large glass dome. And guess what? I was not the only person in the house after all."

"What? What did you see?!"

"In that dim blue light, I saw a woman."

"The woman in the mask."

"Yes. She asked what I was doing and after my explanation, told me that Deb and Ian were gone and weren't coming back."

"Who is this woman?"

"She didn't tell me her name, just that the Garden was her kingdom and she was its queen.

"I explained why we wanted to see Ian and Deb, and told her about the murders and our plans for the Creepers. After briefly considering what I had told her, she said that as the Garden's ruler she would take care of the Creepers. I was instructed to ask everyone to stay inside their cabins that night and the following day; to not leave until the second sunrise, no matter what was heard outside. And, that when we went outside again, the Creepers would be gone. She told me that once this was all done, I should return to her house. Alone."

"And she did what she said?"

"She certainly did. We heard screaming and other terrifying sounds during the following two nights. I stayed with Wolf since my home was in ruins. When we came outside again the Creepers were gone. The only signs they had ever been there were their empty cabins. Even their belongings were gone."

"What did she do to them?"

"I don't know."

"Then you went back to see the woman?"

"I did. She was waiting for me. There was no light to see her with except for the same dim blue glow. She wanted me to deliver a message to the community. To let them know the Garden was hers and that she only allowed them to live there thanks to her…generosity. That no one was to enter her house. No one was to challenge her rule. She heard everything we said and saw everything we did and would let us live in peace as long as we obeyed her rules. If anyone disobeyed, they would be erased from existence just like the Creepers. Over the past few years, a couple of people have been stubborn and tried to enter the house. Neither of them was ever seen again. The bottom line is that if we leave her alone, she leaves us alone."

I should probably be crying. Or feel like all hope is lost. Instead, I just have more questions.

"So this is when my parents disappeared?"

"It is. This was about six years ago."

"I would have been ten."

Cole waited patiently while I absorbed everything. My parents lived here for five years after they disappeared and were presumed dead. They were obviously coming here even before that. Maybe they found a way to come back and forth and then got stuck here like me? I'm still worried that they're dead or suffering, but this is the closest I have ever been to understanding what happened to them.

As much as I need to return home to my aunt, I feel a strong need to stay and find out what happened to my parents. Maybe—just maybe—they're still here somewhere and I'll get to see them again. For the first time since my parents disappeared, I feel optimistic. I have hope.

Chapter 21

The Good Sleep

WHILE EXITING THE FOG WITH Cole, I try to keep my enthusiasm contained. I can't be too optimistic about finding my parents, but I intend to find out what happened to them at the very least.

"Are you sure you don't want to hang out before dinner?" Cole asks when we arrive in front of Rose's cabin.

"I'm just going to relax for a bit."

"All right." His hand grazes mine and briefly comes to rest on my hip. "I'll see you at Lily's later."

"Okay."

He turns away.

"Cole?"

"Yeah?"

"Thank you," I say, sharing my warmest smile.

He smiles back. "You're welcome."

I wait until he's out of sight before returning to Rose's cabin. It seems empty at first, until Flint comes out of the second room and beams at me.

"Hi, Syn!"

"Hi. Are you here by yourself?"

"Not anymore," he says with a laugh, and strolls over to a closet.

I watch him rummage through the closet and remember how scared he and Rose were when I discovered his reptilian skin and tail. Could Flint secretly be a Creeper? Are they afraid he will be banished if anyone finds out? He's a nice kid. I would have enjoyed growing up with a little brother like him and have always wondered whether my parents would have had more kids if they hadn't disappeared. Not just for me. So they'd still have a family after I'm gone.

"Do you want to play Frisbee?" Flint asks, withdrawing a disc from the top shelf of the closet.

"Sure."

We spread out in the open grassy area behind the cabin. Faint voices are resonating from the Square. Flint throws the Frisbee first—straight into the ground. It rolls away from me in an arc. I go fetch it. On the center of the Frisbee are the words *Camp Sunshine*. The name Marcus is written on a strip of masking tape below this.

Camp Sunshine is a day camp back home. A young boy about Flint's age who's named Marcus, lives a couple of blocks away from me. Last summer, his parents asked me to babysit him. I was just out of the hospital and barely able to take care of myself so Aunt Ruth took care of him. He talked about Camp Sunshine non-stop.

"Where did you get this Frisbee?" I ask.

"It was with the supplies the men brought back from one of their runs."

I toss it to Flint. It flies perfectly level and drifts directly to him. He catches it and says, "Nice throw," which it was, though also a fluke.

Flint tosses the Frisbee again and it flies over my head. He apologizes as I chase after it.

"No worries." I toss it back, no better than Flint's last throw.

We toss the Frisbee around for about ten minutes—playing fetch more than catch for the most part—until another boy comes by and takes over for me. I just can't concentrate on throwing, with thoughts of Camp Sunshine on my mind. I walk to the pond, mulling things over.

Flint's Frisbee shows that despite what Rose thinks, the lights in the fog do lead people back to my world. If I'd known this earlier, I would have gone into the light. However, now that I know my parents were here, getting home doesn't seem as important. At least not yet. I decide to rest at the pond before having dinner at Lily's. Then, start searching for information about my parents.

Like at home, this is the place that calms me the best. I kick off my sandals, lie on my back, and wiggle my toes in the water. It's just me, a few ducks in the pond and birds chirping in the trees and shrubs.

I absolutely have to get inside that house. If my parents lived there, some of their belongings are likely still there. For all I know, the masked woman is holding them prisoner. I have to figure out how to get in there without being noticed.

Plus, there are parts of the Garden not explored yet, such as the bog. Seeing what's in there might be a good idea. Maybe Lily or Cole will go down there with me tomorrow. Then I'll figure out how to get inside the house undetected.

My eyes close and I doze for a while. Cole is lying next to me, asleep, when my eyes flutter open. A shiver ripples through my body with the thought of holding his hand, but I decide to just watch him sleep. Even though his appearance is odd, he's a good-looking guy. Very good-looking. I must keep my feelings for him in check though. I'm only here for a short time and don't want to lead him on.

Besides, Cole doesn't know about my illness and though I don't hide it from anyone at home, he has only known me as a healthy young girl. For whatever reason, I'd rather Cole and the others didn't know about all the drugs and treatments I go through every day to keep myself alive. I'm a little ashamed for wanting to keep that a secret because it's always been a part of who I am. I have no idea why I don't want anyone here to know.

Cole's eyes open. "Hey there. How long have you been awake?"

"Not long."

"You could have woken me."

"You could have woken *me*."

"I liked watching you sleep."

"Me too," I say, trying to keep from smiling.

Cole sits up and pulls a timepiece out of his pocket. "Let's head to Lily's place in ten minutes."

We sit silently, watching the ducks in the pond. It's soothing to watch them glide across the surface of the water, dipping occasionally for food. A plane inches across the sky, high enough that there is no sound. All is peaceful, above and below.

Cole stands up and stretches. He crooks his elbow and offers it to me. "Shall we go?"

I stand up and loop my arm in his. Lily and Fern's cabin is on the opposite side of the pond. When we reach the other side, clucking sounds are coming from a small wooden shack with wire fencing surrounding it. It's a chicken coop.

Just past that is a row of several cabins with lots of green space between them. As we approach the second to last cabin, Fern walks out the door.

"You're not staying?" I ask.

"No, no. You young 'uns have fun. Rose is having me over."

We follow the aroma of garlic inside. I hadn't been that hungry, but can't wait to eat now.

Lily pokes her head out from the second room. She is wearing an apron. "Make yourselves at home, guys. I'll be out in a minute."

"It smells great!" I say.

Unsure what to do, I wander around the room. She has different furniture but it's arranged pretty much like Rose's.

Just as she said, Lily appears a minute later. "I'm so glad you're here!"

She motions for us to sit at the table by the window, which is nicely set. Cole and I nibble on garlic bread while Lily runs in and out of the kitchen. She might be around my age but while playing host to our dinner party she demonstrates the maturity of someone older.

The first course is Caesar salad. It's the best salad I've ever had and I tell Lily so. She laughs it off. When we're done eating, I stand up to help her take the empty plates away. She won't hear of it and disappears into the kitchen again.

Cole playfully kicks my feet under the table, apologizes, and then immediately does it again. He must find it pretty amusing. I don't mind. Lily returns with a new set of plates and asks what we're up to. I kick Cole back and we all laugh. She makes several more trips back and forth, bringing a bowl of mashed potatoes, sautéed beets, and a huge pot of beef stew. Cole and I wait until Lily joins us before we begin eating. The food is delicious.

"How did you learn to cook so well?" I ask.

"My mom taught me. We alternate cooking dinner."

"Well, it's super impressive."

I'm about to tell Lily how stuffed I am when she gets up and says she'll bring out dessert. She returns to the kitchen and Cole and I raise our eyebrows at each other. She comes back with a plate of shortbread cookies.

Despite Lily's objections, Cole and I insist on helping clear the table. She refuses to let us wash dishes though and ushers us to the couch in the main room. After Lily goes to the kitchen to get tea, Cole grabs two cookies and shoves them into his pocket.

I giggle quietly. "What are you doing?"

"Trying to save face," Cole murmurs. "I can't speak for you, but my stomach will explode if I eat any more."

Lily returns with a tray holding a pot of tea, a cup of milk, and three mugs. As she sets it on the table she tilts her head at the plate of cookies. "I see you've tried my cookies."

"Hell yeah," Cole says. "They're delicious!"

"So good," I add, trying to contain my laughter.

Lily looks at Cole and then at me, and twists her mouth into a smirk. "That's great," she says. "Please have more. I won't be satisfied until the plate is empty."

Cole and I burst into laughter. Lily laughs too, probably at our silliness. She finally relaxes and the three of us sip tea (though I can barely down any of that either), and talk. There are still many unanswered questions but I enjoy chatting about nothing with Cole and Lily and don't want to wreck the mood. I'm also unsure of which subjects are better discussed in the fog.

The sun has gone down. I didn't even notice until now. We've been here for more than four hours and it's hard to remember what we talked about. What I do know is that I feel like I...belong.

"So what are your plans tomorrow, Syn?" Lily asks.

"I'm thinking about exploring the bog. I haven't done that yet."

Cole and Lily exchange glances.

"You shouldn't go by yourself," Cole says.

"When you're ready," Lily offers, "come find me and we can go together, okay?"

"Sounds good."

Cole seems relieved. I wonder why they are so concerned but don't ask. The door opens and Fern walks in.

"Hi, Mom," Lily says. "How was dinner?"

"It was lovely," Fern says. "How was yours?"

"Fantastic!" exclaims Cole. "You've taught your daughter to be an amazing cook."

"Lily's too humble. She taught herself to be that good. She's a much better cook than I am."

"Well, the food was terrific," I say. "Incredible, actually."

"How about the cookies?"

"They were great too," I fib. "Too bad I only had room for one."

"Well that's interesting," Lily says with a smirk. "It doesn't look like more than a couple are missing from the plate. Plus, I saw Cole stuff two into his pocket."

Busted.

Lily laughs off my explanation, as Cole and I stand up to leave.

"Don't let her rush you out," says Fern.

"Thanks. But it's getting late," notes Cole.

I hug Lily and we say our goodbyes.

When the door closes, Cole takes my hand in his, the warmth enveloping me immediately. The evening is mild and perfect as we walk silently, hand in hand, occasionally smiling at one another.

When we arrive at Rose's cabin, Cole takes my other hand and gently pulls me against him. His big brown eyes with a splash of blue captivate me and I am helpless in his arms. He leans closer, softly stroking my cheek, staring down at my lips. Hearts pounding. We tilt our heads. Close our eyes. Our lips touch.

The kiss is magical. My body tingles from head to toe. I disappear from the Garden. It feels like

I'm in a whole new world, a universe devoid of anyone but Cole. When our lips part, I'm afraid he'll notice my body quivering. We remain lost in each other's eyes until finally, when it feels as if my legs are about to collapse from the excitement, Cole beams at me with delight.

"Goodnight," he mouths.

Leaning against the door for support, I watch him walk away. He turns around, waves, and then disappears into the night.

For the first night since arriving in the Garden, I lie in bed without one thought about returning home. Cole's kiss has charmed me. My first kiss with Jon was nothing like this. It was like Cole has known me forever and knew exactly how to please me. My body tingles again and I have thoughts like I've never had before. Thoughts I won't even let myself admit to. I roll over onto my side and pretend Cole is holding me again. My sinful thoughts evolve into a sense of comfort and belonging. Perhaps Cole is in his bed at this moment imagining me lying beside him. When I'm absolutely sure he is, I imagine him kissing my forehead and fall asleep in perfect bliss.

Chapter 22

Bogged Down

I WAKE UP, COUGHING. Something is resting on my waist. It's Cole's arm. I'm baffled. I had only imagined him sleeping next to me—right?

Cole mumbles incoherently as I look around. This isn't Rose's cabin. I'm in my bedroom at home! Phlegm is building up in my throat. Oh, god! Did I dream the whole thing?

That would make sense only if Cole weren't in my bed. Trying to stifle another cough, I reach for my inhaler. It's not on the night table. I cough frantically. My bedroom door opens and Aunt Ruth walks in.

"Are you okay Syn, what—" She sees Cole in bed beside me and one hand rushes to her dropped jaw.

Coughing uncontrollably, I drop my feet onto the floor. They get caught in the sheet and I fall out of bed. As I thunk onto the floor, my eyes open wide.

I *was* dreaming. I'm on the wooden floor of Rose's cabin. There is no phlegm in my throat and I'm not coughing. But is—? I scramble to my knees and sigh with relief. The bed is empty. Sunlight is beaming through the window. Shockingly, it's just past eleven in the morning. How embarrassing that the comfort of Cole's imagined embrace may have caused me to sleep in.

Neither Rose nor Flint is home. I take some slices of cheese from the fridge and a couple of pieces of bread from the bread box, and smack them together. I eat the sandwich standing up, gazing out the window. Then, I wash it down with a glass of milk and take a quick shower.

After my shower, I dry off, get dressed, brush my teeth, and see that it's 11:45. Guess my shower wasn't that quick. I am just about to walk out the door when Rose and Flint arrive.

"She's awake. Finally!" Flint chirps with a mischievous smile.

"I'm a little embarrassed about sleeping in."

"Don't be," Rose says. "You must have had some pretty sweet dreams."

My face is surely turning red. Even though it's ridiculous, I can't help but think Rose knows something about last night.

She laughs. "Just teasing. We came for some lunch. Do you want anything?"

"I just had a bite, thanks."

Rose and Flint are walking into the second room when Rose spins around. "I just remembered! Lily came by to see you. She can't go to the bog today. Her mother needs help with something. She can go tomorrow though."

That's disappointing. The bog is the only area of the Garden I haven't explored except for inside that house, and I haven't built up the courage to go there again.

"Thanks for telling me."

"You shouldn't go to the bog by yourself. If you really want to explore it today, I'm sure Cole would be happy to go with you."

I smile at the thought. "Good idea. See you in a while." I leave the cabin and am bathed in warm sunshine and fresh, natural scents.

While basking in the sunshine and admiring the greenery, I recall the dream from last night…and Cole's *amazing* kiss. Though it seems like it's been longer, Jon only broke up with me a few days ago. And since I'm only staying in the Garden longer to find out about my parents, I don't plan on being here permanently. Maybe Cole would come back with me. This is just too much to think about now. I have a mission and can't let Cole distract me. The bog awaits.

I cross paths with a few other travelers. Their faces look familiar but their names have been erased from my memory. We simply nod to each other, equally intent on reaching our destinations.

There is a distinct sound of bugs buzzing, crickets chirping, and frogs croaking, which increases as I approach the bog. Ferns, shrubs, and trees growing berries define its perimeter. A path has been cleared through the center. I move off the grass onto the soft, beige peat moss and amble down the spongy path, keeping an eye out for clues. It's doubtful there will be anything related to my parents but I need to be thorough just in case.

A juicy-looking blackberry catches my eye, however a spider is sitting in the center of its web, which is woven in-between the branches. I don't want to destroy its hard work. Most people don't have the same appreciation for spiders that I do. A spider builds its home in the morning and sits there patiently, still and silent all day, waiting for a bug to fly into its web. Sometimes this doesn't happen and they eat nothing that day. Other times, a person, another creature, or the weather destroys the web. The spider will again go a day without food and rebuild its home from scratch in the morning. It's not an easy life and I respect that. I pull a berry off another bush and pop it in my mouth. It's sweeter than the blackberries I've had at home.

Proceeding through the bog, I reach a two-pronged fork. The route to the left looks similar to this path. A battered wooden fence separates the path from swampland adjacent to the path on the right. That direction seems more interesting. I'll explore the other path later.

The fence is made of two horizontal logs with a gap between them large enough for a kid to climb through easily. Swamp water beyond the fence is heavily populated with dragonflies and frogs and is surrounded by a muddy shore. The bog is totally different from the pristine feel of the Garden. Still, I can't help enjoy its natural, rustic quality and the humming of bugs and croaking of frogs.

A short distance later I stop suddenly, my ears perked at the sound of someone in distress. It sounds like a child crying, but after advancing closer it becomes clear that it's a bird. My pace quickens until I realize the sound is getting farther away. Backtracking and listening carefully, I find the spot on the path where the wailing sounds the loudest, though there is no sign of anything.

The area beyond the fence is mostly swamp water, and home to croaking frogs that skillfully remain inconspicuous. Large rocks randomly jut above the water and the muddy shore. Frantic, my eyes dart here and there. Finally I see it. A small bird, possibly a robin, is in the mud, flailing one of its wings. Either a leg or the other wing is stuck in the mud or under something.

There are only two options to save the bird. Follow the path to see if a branch of it leads to the muddy area, or climb over the fence. Searching for another path could take too long and I might get lost, so that's not the best idea. Climbing the fence and jumping across the rocks to reach the bird seems like the best choice. Some of the rocks are spaced far apart, but this seems doable. Some would say there's a third option, but leaving the bird to die isn't something I would even consider. All life is sacred. And in this Garden world, it probably wouldn't die anyway but would be in torment for eternity, a fate even worse than death.

Straddling the fence and hopping down onto the narrow ledge of dirt beside the water is the easy part. I jump onto a rock, then a second rock, wobbling but managing to keep my balance. The next rock is so small only one foot will fit on it. However, it's close enough to stretch my leg to without jumping and there's just a short stride from that rock to a larger one, which would bring me very close to the bird. The larger rock is slimy and my foot slips. Waving my arms frantically, I'm able to steady myself. My sandal is wet but luckily I didn't fall in!

Upon closer inspection, I see the bird's red belly, confirming it is a robin, and in peril. Its wing is indeed stuck in the mud. The poor thing is watching me, like it's pleading for help.

"Almost there. I'm going to get you out."

The next rock is just one long step away. My foot slides out from under me the instant I step onto it. I almost do the splits and fall sideways into the mucky water. In my favor, it turns out to be quite shallow, no more than two feet deep. I'm covered in sludge but can easily walk through the swamp without having to leap over more rocks.

The poor bird seems more frightened than ever with me towering over it. I sit on a log and gently touch the bird's wing. It's not exactly mud that the bird's wing is stuck in but rather, some strange tarlike substance. It's extremely sticky. Splashing water on the wing has the bird flailing in panic. In a minute its fear will be gone and it will be free. I splash more water on the wing and then carefully use my fingers to inch it out of the sludge. More muck should be removed from the wing but as soon as the bird is free, it flaps its wings and flies away.

I'm all wet and muddy, my hands are sticky with sludge, but I feel fantastic! I saved the bird's life.

After resting on the log for a moment and enjoying a celebratory moment, I stand up and am about to walk back across the shallow pond when something in the sky catches my eye.

In the sky, perhaps above the Square, an object is flailing about as it descends rapidly. A kite in free-fall? No, it's not an object at all. It's a person! In just seconds, the figure appears larger and larger. I take a few steps toward where it is falling, even though it will be out of my sightline momentarily. Big mistake.

Immediately my feet sink. And keep sinking! The mud is a sludgy quicksand, and is dragging me down into it. I grab for the log but the more I move, the faster it pulls me down. If I don't think of something soon, I'll be completely swallowed up.

"Help!" I yell as loudly as possible. "Help! I'm stuck! Help me!"

My hands slide from the log as the sludge drags me away. I gulp air before my mouth is covered by the mud, and close my eyes. Sunlight shines through my eyelids for a moment. Seconds later everything goes black.

Chapter 23

Beneath the Garden

IF MY SITUATION WASN'T SO dire, I might laugh at the irony. A girl whose life was destined to be cut short finds a place where she can live forever, only to find herself buried alive years before her time has come.

Now that I'm completely buried and can no longer breathe, not doing anything would be admitting defeat. I won't just give up. I push my arms and legs out as far as possible through the sludge and surprisingly, feel something. Against the tip of the longest finger on my right hand. Something cool. Air.

Can't hold my breath much longer. Pushing my body to the right with every ounce of strength. Soon one foot is free. Then the rest of my leg. My mind is slipping away as I desperately drag myself through the mud. Cool air touches the tip of my nose. With one final attempt, I push my head forward another inch and am able to breathe through my nose. I can't open my eyes because of all the muck so it's not possible to see where I am. At least I'm not going to die. Not yet anyway.

My chest heaves, gasping for air. After taking a moment to compose myself, I doggedly shove ahead until my face is completely out of the mud. Then my shoulders and chest. My left arm. In the process of freeing my left leg I drop about a foot down into shallow water. Mud slurps into my mouth. This doesn't bother me. I'm free. Alive!

I give myself a moment to lie in the shallow pool of water and regain some strength. The air is cool and carries a musty stench. I rinse my hands in the water, splash it over my face, wipe the tarry substance off my eyelids and open my eyes.

This is a tunnel. A sewer, actually. There is a flickering light in the distance, enough that I'm able to see that the water is brown and flows along the center of the tunnel. The foul odor is similar to what a downtown alley might smell like after a rainfall. There are higher platforms and rusty metal pipes on either side of the tunnel. The passage goes on for as far as the eye can see.

I stand up and turn around, soaking wet and still very dirty. There is nothing but a wall of mud behind me. In the few minutes since falling down here, the gap I came through has filled in. It's as if it was never there.

Although I'm surprised by my surroundings, it makes sense that there is a sewer line underneath the Garden. And yet there is no sound of water flowing through the pipes. Except for the sound of water dripping, it's perfectly quiet down here.

After rinsing off as much of the mud as possible, I wring out my wet hair like a mop and disgusting black water flows out. My hair is hopeless at this point. Most of the guck comes off my skin though. I hope Lily's outfit isn't ruined.

The thought of the figure falling from the sky haunts me. Where could someone have possibly fallen from? The stairway is at the opposite end of the Garden and I didn't see any planes in the sky. Would the Garden help the person survive and heal if they slammed into the ground? Or will there soon be a new mound of dirt in the cemetery by the house?

I force these morbid thoughts out of my head, unable to do anything about this right now. My immediate goal is to find a way back to the surface. There has to be a ladder somewhere. I climb onto the concrete platform to avoid trekking through dirty water. My footsteps echo off the walls of the tunnel for a few minutes. I approach the flickering light, a lantern mounted to the concrete wall. It allows me to see that another tunnel is coming up on my left.

Cautiously, I peer into the new tunnel. It is similar to this one, except that in the distance there are more openings on each side. One quick glance down the tunnel I'm in reveals at least two more openings in the distance.

So many options. I try to determine my location in relation to the Garden above me, visualizing the map I sketched. It would seem that I'm slightly past the entrance to the bog. The left turn might take me to the staircase. If so, going forward would lead in the direction of the Square. Perhaps I can get to the surface through the well if there is a connection to these tunnels. What other area of the Garden might lead down here? Leaving the way I came isn't an option.

I move on. Just as that tunnel in question is out of sight, there is a splashing sound from that direction. I stop, hold my breath. Nothing more to hear and nothing moving ahead of me either. I step forward again and hear another splash...and footsteps! Hurrying, almost running, I turn around occasionally and see nothing.

In-between the echoes of my brisk footsteps my ears tune into the sound of voices. Or, whispers. It's not easy to make out the words. They might be vibrating through the pipes. I convince myself that they're traveling through the pipes from the Garden above.

Another tunnel appears on my left. I peer into the opening and hear pitter-patters on the water. There is definitely something down there. Goosebumps sprout on my arms as I creep away.

Up ahead is a black metal slab against the brick wall, which looks like a door. The voices seem to get louder as I approach, though it's still not possible to make out what they're saying. The metal slab is indeed a door. Maybe it leads to a ladder! The heavy door creaks loudly as I tug on it, stepping off the platform and into the murky water to pull it all the way open.

Through the door is a small concrete room. There is a table against a wall, with a chair tucked under it. On the wall over the table are a couple of framed photographs. One is of a botanical garden very similar to the Garden above, and the other is of a bear standing over a waterfall with a fish in its mouth.

In a far corner of the room is an unmade bed. Lying on the bed is a man who is staring at me with perplexed wide eyes. He's wearing headphones that are attached to a yellow, old-fashioned cassette player in his lap. He seems to be in his mid-forties, has a thin face with a bit of stubble, and messy salt and pepper hair.

"Who are you?" he asks loudly. He takes off his headphones and sits up. "You shouldn't be down here."

I'm not certain whether he's friendly or not but the surprise of seeing him frightens me. I back out of the room and run down the tunnel, leaving the heavy door open.

"Wait! Don't go!" His voice soon bounces off the walls of the tunnel.

Water splashes around my feet as I tear past more metal doors, not daring to open them. Eventually the tunnel dead-ends at a brick wall. But before the brick wall is a tunnel on the left. Even though there's a lantern flickering in the distance, it's still too dark to see what's down there.

Heavy splashing sounds coming from behind send me spinning round on my heels. Two scaly creatures are in hot pursuit. Behind them are smaller creatures that are nothing but shadows in the dark tunnel. I bolt in the direction of the flickering light and hope for the best.

As I sprint for my life, multitudes of voices are chattering incoherently from every direction. A hasty glance behind reveals shadows are chasing me. I pass another metal door with a lantern next to it. I'm just strides away from a T, with the option to go left or right. Which way? There are no more lit lanterns in this tunnel, while faint light is shining from the two corridors at the T.

Thirty seconds from the end of the tunnel, I dare to glance back. The creatures are gaining on me! As I blindly dart through the tunnel, I smack into something hard, rebound a few feet, and stop. I'm stuck!

My body is facing the T. My head is stuck sideways. Flailing around doesn't help. I press my hands against whatever is holding me, trying to figure out what it is. Now my hands are stuck too.

Out of the corner of my eye, I see two huge shadowy creatures and what looks like two dogs approaching. One of the creatures lights a torch with a match. They both stand upright and each has a long tail and the face of a crocodile. The dog-like creatures look exactly like dogs, except that they are covered in green scales. Creepers!

One of the Creepers clutches my chin between his scaly fingers and sniffs my face. "What do we have here?" he asks in a deep voice.

"Looks like dinner to me," replies the other crocodile-faced Creeper.

I start shaking so hard that whatever I'm stuck to vibrates.

The pair backs away from me with alarm. A shadow passes above—the gigantic shadow of a spider. It must be crawling in front of a lantern. No insect is that large.

"Hands off," says a woman's voice from above. "I caught it, so it's mine."

Terrified, almost paralyzed, I manage to tilt my neck back far enough to see what is above. It's a spider alright—if one could even call it that—an enormous version of the spider-boy. This one has the face of a woman, two pairs of human arms and legs, and the human flesh-covered body of a spider. A thing of nightmares. With a jolt, I realize what I'm stuck to—her web!

The giant spider-woman lowers herself on her web so that her eyes glare directly into mine. She smiles an upside down smile through pretty lips and scary-as-hell sharp, yellow teeth. "Why, child, don't you look delicious."

Chapter 24

A Synful Delicacy

THE SPIDER-WOMAN SLIDES down her web and hovers over me. Probably taking inventory of the meat she can glean from her captured prey. I'm going to throw up.

"We saw her first," one of the crocodilian Creepers protests.

The spider-woman shoots a web to the tunnel's ceiling and disappears. Her voice echoes from above us. "Am I going to have to call my mate?"

The crocodile men retreat. "That won't be necessary. Enjoy your meal."

The spider-woman drops down to face me again. "Now you're all mine."

Faces flash before my eyes. Janna. Aunt Ruth, Cole. My parents. I have never felt fear like in this instant. Not even when I almost drowned or while buried in the mud. Being eaten alive, by a creature that defies reason, is up there with the most painful ways a person could die.

"P-please. P-p-please don't hurt me."

"Oh, how cute. It's begging."

Shaking uncontrollably, I can hardly speak. "I j-just want to go b-back. T-to the Garden."

"How ironic. One of *you* begging one of *us* to return to the surface. When it was us down on our knees—so to speak—begging to return to *our* homes, your queen wouldn't hear a word of it, would she?"

"M-my queen?"

"Sinister."

"I d-don't know what you're t-talking about."

The spider-woman leans in and stares me dead in the eyes. "Who are you? What are you doing down here?"

"M-my name is Syn. I w-was exploring the bog. S-sunk into some m-mud. And ended up here."

Her eyes seem to penetrate me. "What were you looking for?"

"I t-think my parents were h-here. They went missing when I was little."

The spider-woman rolls her eyes and shoots back up to the ceiling. She slides down on a new strand, leaving more space between us. "You're not from the Garden, are you?"

"No," I say, a little less scared now that she's not so close. "I only got here a few days ago."

"Interesting. Very interesting. Hang on a minute." The spider-woman smirks. "Not that you have a choice."

The spider-woman disappears again and a moment later, shouts down the corridor, "If anyone else tries to eat you, tell them Maya has a claim on you."

I don't know what to think. My fate is still up in the air but a little optimism glimmers inside me. Besides that, a small part of me is laughing after hearing that this terrifying creature is named Maya.

Soon my ears tune into skittering noises behind me. Maya drops down in front of me. On each side of her are five much smaller human/spider creatures, all children, like the spider-boy I saw at the pond. Four of them are male and one is female. In fact, I'm pretty sure one of the males *is* the spider-boy I saw!

"She looks very juicy, Mom," the girl says.

"Hold your horses, Tasha," Maya says. "Jeremy, is this the girl you saw in the Garden?"

Jeremy adjusts himself on his silken thread to face me. "Yes. That's her, Mother."

"Well, dear Syn," Maya says, "we have quite a dilemma. The variety of food down here is limited, to say the least. You would be a delicious treat for my family."

I don't like the sound of this.

"However," Maya continues, "I have lost too many children to those monsters above. They stomp on my offspring like they are nothing. It seems, however, that *you* were kind to my son. Why is that?"

"I try my best to be kind to everyone. I would never kill another creature. Life is too precious."

"You are an interesting child, young Syn. You're new here and can't be blamed like the others."

"So you're not going to eat me?" I ask in a hopeful, squeaky voice.

"I didn't say that. If I deny your juices to my children you must give us something in return."

"I'll do anything. Anything!"

"I bet you would." Maya nods at her children. "Cut her down, little ones. If she runs, we'll web her mouth shut and suck her dry."

My stomach churns.

Her children jump onto the web and it starts to sag. I fall into shallow, mucky water. Sticky strands of spider web cling to me everywhere. There isn't enough time to brush it all off my face before Maya jumps to the ground.

She stands on her four hind legs, her kids hanging from silken threads beside her. "So, young Syn, do you know anything about us?"

"You're Creepers?"

"That's an offensive designation, but yes, you are correct. If you've been told about us, I assume you know why we're here."

"You lived with the people above peacefully. Then you were banished. After some of you, um…"

"After some of us what?"

"Um, did some, uh, bad things."

"Bad things?"

"Killed people."

"Yes." Maya nods. "That is what they believe above. It is not the truth. None of us murdered anyone."

"Then who did?"

"Well, isn't that the question of the decade?"

"Can't you just go up there and tell them that none of you killed anyone? Maybe you can find out who did?"

"Unfortunately, it's not that easy. Have you met Sinister?"

"Sinister?"

"The woman who secludes herself in the large house."

"No. I only saw her through a window."

"She activated a signal that emits a high-pitched frequency. The humans can't hear it. In fact, it's a frequency that is so specific only we Creepers who were here in the Garden at the time it was created, are affected."

"Affected?"

"Yes. It makes us gravely ill, very quickly. We begin to bleed from our ears, noses, and even our pores. It feels like our heads will explode. If we are out there long enough, they surely will."

"That's horrible," I say, sincerely.

"Yes, it is. I'm glad to hear that you sympathize with our situation."

"What do you want me to do?"

"My children aren't affected by the frequency because they were born in the Garden afterward. They have scoured the land above in search of the source of the signal. Many have lost their lives in hopes of ending our nightmare, hopes that have so far been unfulfilled. However, just last week my daughter Mavis was hiding inside Sinister's house. She thinks she found a box with the technology that emits the frequency. It's a glass box that glows bright yellow. I want you to find this box and destroy the machine inside. You will do this for us in exchange for your life."

I nod solemnly. "But only if you promise not to harm any of the people above when you return to the surface."

Maya's eyes pierce mine. "After what they have done? I will not agree to that."

"Then we don't have a deal."

Maya bares her yellow teeth and leans in. "Then we will rip you apart, suck the juices from your belly and the marrow from your bones."

I put on a brave face, despite feeling anything but brave. "Then I hope I taste good."

Maya looks truly shocked. "You would give your life for those monsters?"

"Life is precious," I say. "All life."

Maya stares at me for some time. Analyzing me. Contemplating. "You are a brave girl, young Syn," she finally says. "You are also our only hope.

I give you my word—I will make sure no one above us is harmed."

I am suspicious, but she sounds sincere. Her hatred of Sinister is certainly a point in her favor. "We have a deal."

Maya glances at my outstretched hand and then at me. "What are you doing?"

"Let's shake on it."

Maya laughs. "You humans have the most ridiculous customs. Let's get you home."

Chapter 25

The Swarm

MAYA ESCORTS ME DOWN THE tunnel. As we turn a corner, I feel light vibrations beneath my feet.

"What's that?"

"Come along and I'll show you," Maya says. "I hope you're not squeamish."

As we move through the long sewer tunnel, the vibrations increase. Maya descends on a thread and peers through a window at the top of a metal door.

"I'm getting hungry just being here," Maya says. She moves out of the way and motions for me to take a look. Standing on my toes, I peer through the window and immediately spring backward upon seeing what's inside. Hundreds of large rats are jammed into the confined space. The floor is completely packed with them, and they are crawling on top of one another.

"What is—?"

Maya snickers. "That's breakfast, lunch, and dinner."

"You…eat *them*?"

"Since we can't go above ground there's nothing else to eat. We are carnivores and breeding rats was the only alternative to eating each other. Having the same thing to eat every day gets dull very fast. Your meat would have been a delicious change, but that isn't in the cards."

"Thank god," I say louder than intended.

Maya studies me. "That's enough of that. Let's go."

We march through more tunnels. A man with thinning hair becomes visible in the shadows, startling me. Writhing on the ground in front of him are three extraordinarily long snakes. Not regular snakes, Creeper snakes with humanlike flesh instead of scales. They seem…excited…to see me.

"What do we have here?" the man mumbles. A forked tongue slithers from his mouth and then snaps back inside.

In the blink of an eye, Maya's web descends from the ceiling and dangles in-between me and the Creepers. "She's mine."

Disappointed, the man and the snake creatures pass by us without another word. I dare turn around to watch them. The man is staring at me, licking his lips with his snakelike tongue. I shiver as their shadowy figures merge with the darkness.

Maya leads me into another tunnel. My neck is getting sore from looking up at her crawling above me on the ceiling. After walking for what seems like hours, we stop at a dead end, at a wall made out of mud, just like the one I came through.

"We're here," Maya says as she drops onto her hind legs in front of me.

"Through the mud?"

"No, silly girl." Maya gestures up to the concrete ceiling, to a metal sewer lid. "That will take you above ground."

Maya jumps to the ceiling and sinks to the platform beside me, leaving a thread of web stretching up to the lid. She repeats this many more times, then weaves all the threads together into one thick strand. I watch curiously, as she spits on her hands and feet and rubs them all over the web.

"That's all I can do for you, child. You'll need to open that sucker on your own. If I'm nearby when you open it, I'll be tormented by the frequency. Please do make sure to put it back in place once you've climbed out."

"It looks heavy."

"I'm sure it is."

"Won't my hands stick to the web?"

Maya smiles. "Do you think I spit on my hands for your amusement? Worst-case scenario, you'll stick to it and I'll feed your juices to my children."

Her humor is a tad dark for my taste.

Maya leaps to the ceiling and crawls in the direction we came from. "You will keep your promise to me now, won't you, girl?" she calls without looking back.

I nod, even though she can't see. "And you'll keep yours? No one will get hurt?"

"That was our agreement, was it not?" Maya disappears around the corner. From a distance, I hear her for the last time. "Take care of yourself, young Syn."

Reminding myself to breathe, I grip Maya's web rope tightly with both hands. It's slippery. The kids at my school climbed rope in gym class, except for me, because of my CF. It looked like fun from the bleachers. Now is my chance. I wrap my legs around the rope and gradually pull myself up, breathless upon reaching the top. When reaching out one hand to touch the lid—whoosh—I slide down again, my butt splashing to a hard landing in the shallow water.

Off come my sandals. I stick my hands through the straps so they hang on my arms. They belong to Lily so I can't just leave them behind. At the top again, bare feet give me enough traction to let go with one hand and touch the lid. I slip a bit, but only an inch or two. Now, with both hands pushing, the lid moves slightly. Sadly, not enough to let any light through. I try again, using every bit of strength that's left. It budges a little, just enough to push it to the side an inch or so before my legs lose their grip and I slide down again, gritting my teeth in anticipation of another hard landing. I stand up defiantly. After a couple more unwelcome dips in the water, I manage to shove the lid far enough to create a gap big enough to squeeze through.

With some hesitation, I hoist myself through the narrow opening and hug the ground like a long-lost friend. I'm in the fog. A familiar light flashes in the distance. As Maya instructed, I shove the sewer lid in place, then slip the sandals from my arms. Heading in the opposite direction to the flash, it feels good to be wearing Lily's sandals again.

Passing through the wall of fog, I welcome the fresh air and all the color that surrounds me. Even though some of the Creepers wanted to eat me, it's still sad that they have to live in such a dank place with nothing to eat but rats.

I walk for a few minutes, trying to collect my thoughts. Voices are chattering up ahead and soon my path brings me to the Square where about ten people are either serving food from the harvest or collecting it. I wave and move briskly through the Square.

The blonde-haired girl who was playing ball with Flint just after I found the spider-boy strolls past, moving in the opposite direction.

"Hey!"

She turns around.

"Can I ask you something?"

"Sure."

"I was just in the bog and saw something fall from the sky. It looked like a person."

"Yeah. It was a man. Some of the grown-ups buried him in the fog."

So I really did see a man fall from the sky. To his death.

"Where did he fall from?"

The girl squints at me. "The sky, of course. Where do people fall from where you come from?"

She walks away from my bewildered expression. What kind of crazy world am I in where people fall from the sky and it's considered a normal, everyday occurrence? Though I did just make a deal with a talking human-spider hybrid, didn't I? Not to mention, in this world a sick girl can become perfectly healthy in an instant. Yet another reason to find some answers.

I eagerly scrub all the grime off in Rose's shower. It's a relief to watch the muck disappear down the drain, as well as to be safely out of those tunnels and not stuck in some giant spider's web negotiating for my life!

Feeling clean and refreshed, and dressed in another one of Lily's outfits, I consider putting off sneaking into Sinister's house today. The clock reads 2:37. Plenty of time to find Cole and enjoy the afternoon, then worry about that tomorrow. But it's not something I'll look forward to tomorrow either. Better to just get it over with.

While approaching Cole's cabin on my way to
the pond, I put my head down and pick up speed.
Although it would be great to see him, now is not
the time. As fate would have it, just as I pass his
cabin the door opens and he appears. At the
instant recollection of our kiss, my knees grow
weak.

"Syn!" he says. "You trying to sneak past me?"

"Of course not," I lie. "Rose asked me to find
Flint and give him a message."

He takes both of my hands in his. "Okay. I
won't keep you then. I'd like to spend some time
with you, though. Maybe this evening?"

I smile. "Yeah, this evening would be good."

Cole leans in with twinkling eyes and gives me
a soft kiss on the lips. The warmth that flows
through me invites a strong yearning for this
evening. He lets go of my hands and we each
move on with our business. When I glance over
my shoulder, Cole is standing on his doorstep,
watching me. My heart leaps and I manage a wave
without staggering on legs that still feel like jelly.
Cole's dazzling smile follows me the rest of the
way to the pond.

Rather than following the path from the pond,
I decide to take another route to the house. A
route that could get me inside without being seen.
Four people are working among the trees in the
orchard, including Lily and her mom. I figure it's

better to act normal than to try to sneak by and arouse suspicion.

Fern is handing apples down to Lily, who is putting them in a basket. Lily waves. I wave and keep moving before she has a chance to gesture for me to come over. At the end of the orchard, I scan around for prying eyes. Satisfied that I'm alone, I walk into the fog.

Hugging the border of the Garden, I move north. Just beyond the fog should be the large grassy field to the left of the house. Suspecting I've reached the northwest corner, my path veers to the right and goes for about a minute. Then I stop. If spotted, my advantage is lost. If that happens, I'll spend the afternoon with Cole and try again tomorrow. I'm playing a game of chance.

I peek through the border of the fog into the Garden and look around. There is no one in the field. From my vantage point, it appears that all the windows of the house are covered. Crouching slightly, a diagonal sprint across the field brings me safely to the side of the house. There's no sign of anyone, especially anyone peering through the curtains. With my back touching the outside of the carport, I slink along the wall to the basement windows at the back. They are covered. Good!

While sliding along the back of the house, I feel mildly dizzy. The graveyard is having its effect again, even though it's farther away than before. This has to be done quickly so my focus isn't lost.

At the foot of the staircase, off come the sandals. After carefully sliding them past my wrists, I rapidly ascend the stairs on tiptoes, my eyes fixed on the covered windows. The voices in my head have started again but they fade away as I move farther up the stairs. The dizziness fades as well.

The back door is ajar. It's great that I won't have to climb through a window, but the open door makes me worry that this is a trap. I push through the doorway slowly, hoping to god the hinges don't squeak, and squeeze through the gap with relief that they didn't. It's extremely dark inside except for the meager ray of sunlight peeking through the thick curtains and a dim, blue glow from a large glass dome on the floor.

No one seems to be home. Good. Time to get to work.

Chapter 26

The Basement

DESPITE THE DIM LIGHT, the floorplan is easy to follow. Like Cole said, the space isn't divided into separate rooms. Still it's like being in the same building as the house I grew up in. This is where the kitchen would be but there are no counters or appliances, only long wooden tables holding a dozen or so old PC computers. The equipment looks familiar and that likely isn't a coincidence. The stairwell is in the same location as in my house. A light is shining from a room on the second floor. That Sinister woman is probably up there right now. Assuming the upstairs floor is the same as when Cole came through the house—just bedrooms and bathrooms—there's nothing up there that needs to be scoped out.

There are two reasons I'm here. To find and destroy the device that keeps the Creepers underground, and of course, to find information about my parents. Or even better, to actually find them alive, though it's best to not get my hopes up. The first priority is my parents, but as soon as I stop that frequency for Maya, Sinister will be alerted and I'll need to get out fast.

To my right is a doorway that opens to a staircase. At home, a door leads down to the basement. It's always locked. Before my parents disappeared, the basement was their private area. I remember hearing beeps, sizzles, and loud bangs coming from down there. Sure, I was curious, but I was also young and didn't question their requests for me to stay out. After they disappeared, Aunt Ruth kept the basement locked, untouched; optimistically ready for their return someday. With only two of us in the house, it wasn't like we needed the extra space. When I was twelve, I asked my aunt to let me see what my parents kept down there. We explored the basement together.

It contained old computers similar to the ones in this house. There were layers of dust on everything. Now that I think about it, we saw a small dome, like a desktop, globe-sized version of the big blue one that's here. It wasn't turned on and didn't glow so it's hard to recall if it was any particular color.

I creep over to the stairs, hold onto the railing tightly, and descend into darkness. At the bottom, light seeping in from outside is minimal but enough to light my way.

There is no computer equipment down here. Instead, there are several tables and dozens of storage boxes. I walk over to a table, reach into a couple of the boxes, and feel around. They contain stacks of paper. Picking up a few sheets from the top of one box, I move closer to the window to read. At the top of the first document a date is written—March 22, 2002—and it's titled "Light Transfer Study 881." Beneath the title is written "Conducted by M. Winters." Masie Winters was my parents' research partner. The three of them taught and conducted research at the local college. I don't know what Masie's field was but my mom was in biotech and my dad was a physicist.

I can't make heads or tails of these documents and return them to the box. Most of the storage boxes are labelled "M. Winters." Investigating further, I find a few boxes labelled "I. Wade" and "D. Wade."

Now I'm getting somewhere.

Grabbing a stepstool to use as a chair, I perch next to a box labelled with my father's initials and withdraw a thick stack of papers held together with a large metal clip. This intrigues me, not because of the title of the study—"Stem Cell Reproduction Test Case 492"—or the results, which I would not be able to understand for the life of me. What is intriguing and gives me a sliver of hope is the date on the front page of the study—November 22, 2008. Four years after my parents disappeared. Years after the burned bodies were found. This proves that not only were the police wrong that those burned bodies were my parents, but it confirms they were in this Garden at some point after disappearing.

With my dad's study tucked under my right arm, I reach into a box labeled with my mom's name. Inside is a smaller stack of clipped papers from 2007.

This is enough! If I stay too long in this basement my luck is bound to run out. I'll take the studies with me and try to make sense of them later.

I tiptoe up the dark stairwell hoping the masked woman isn't waiting at the top. The main floor is still deserted.

Now it's time to keep my promise to Maya.

Maya said to look for a small, yellow, glowing glass box. You'd think it would stand out in the dim light but there is nothing resembling that anywhere. I walk past the north wall of the house, where the majority of the screens, keyboards, and control panels are, examining everything thoroughly. The only thing glowing is the large blue dome.

The dome emits a low blue light and what looks like steam. It's sitting on a platform with four legs bolted to the hardwood floor and is humming at a low frequency. What could its purpose be? As I raise my hand above it, sparks shoot from the center to where my palm is hovering. I move my hand closer to the glass, curious to see if the sparks will intensify.

Suddenly, there is a loud bang. A beam of bright light hits me, blinding me for a moment. The light is coming from the front doors, which are now wide open.

"Step away from that." The woman's voice is hoarse, like she has a bad cold.

Sinister is standing at the top of the basement staircase. In the glaring light, only the outline of her body is visible. The two creatures that chased me a few days ago are standing on either side of her, growling.

"You shouldn't sneak into other people's homes, Synthia Wade."

She knows my name. *How does she know my name?!*

"If I found you here a couple of days from now, you'd get a grand welcome. But things aren't ready yet. So you need to leave. Now!"

The growling of the reptile-dog creatures intensifies. I step backward, trip, and fall to the dusty floor. That's when I see it. Attached to the underside of the platform holding up the glowing blue dome is a smaller yellow dome.

The reptile-dogs are almost on top of me. I manage to scramble to my feet and run around the dome with the creatures close behind. Sinister has disappeared. I make a beeline to the front door with the creatures—her pet Creepers—nipping at my heels.

Darting across the front lawn, the Creepers still on my tail, the documents slip from under my arm onto the grass. With the Creepers so close behind, I have no chance to scoop them up. And even worse, escaping into the fog is my only hope.

Narrowly dodging trees that seem to pop up out of nowhere, I realize I'm heading straight toward white flashes of light. Both creatures are closing in, flanking me, herding me to the light. The last time this happened that girl called them off and prevented a mauling.

"Help!"

There is no response other than the Creepers' snarls.

I'm almost under the flashing light. Wait! The chances this light will take me home are slim. Besides, I'm too close to finding out about my parents to leave now. Determined, I decide to double back and race to the Garden, surprising the dogs and halting them in their tracks. Just as I plant my foot to dodge in-between them, a white light flashes directly on me like a spotlight on a stage actor.

Time seems to slow down. Everything is moving in slow motion. Dreamily, I turn my head. The Creepers are crouched behind me. Watching. The light intensifies and where there used to be endless gray fog there is now endless whiteness.

Gradually the whiteness fades. The feeling of moving in slow motion ceases. I'm on a farm. A blueberry farm. Standing behind my neighbor's house. The Sanders' farm back home, a one-minute walk from my house!

Dammit! I was so close to finding out about my parents. Will I ever see Cole, Rose, Flint and Lily again? Here I am, almost home and sadness has encompassed me. Perhaps I'm still in the Garden. Maybe there's a part of the Garden that's similar to the Sanders' farm, just like the pond and the house are similar to my family's property.

I cover my mouth to cough. Phlegm is building in my lungs and throat. Then more coughing. Without a doubt, I've returned home.

Chapter 27

There's No Place Like Home

HEAVING, AND BOLTING THROUGH the blueberry field, past the Sanders' house, I worsen with every step. The full extent of my untreated CF has returned. My illness is bound to hit me hard because there haven't been any treatments for several days. I might not survive if I don't get help soon. Breathless. Hacking. Must get to my house. Find someone to call 911.

When I get to the road, the hacking is so bad I have to stop running. Clutching my chest, I gaze with fondness at my house. A bittersweet homecoming. I bend over, coughing and coughing. Blood splatters on the asphalt. My nose is dripping. My chest feels like it's weighted down with iron plates. Every instinct screams that I should collapse on the street and rest. But that would be it. There would be no getting up.

I force myself to hobble to our front lawn, stopping to hack up more blood. There's no sign of Aunt Ruth's concerned face at the window. I drag myself up the brick steps to the front door. It's slightly ajar. Falling to my knees. Reaching to the doorbell. Must alert Aunt Ruth. Too much phlegm in my throat to yell. I push the door open wider and crawl inside.

Something is wrong. I don't recognize the door mat my coughing is splattering blood onto. The painting on the wall of the foyer hasn't been hanging there since I was a little kid. And the kitchen! I can only see the floor and counter through the open door ahead but the linoleum floor has a yellow and orange checkered pattern. The cupboards are orange and the counter is light yellow. This is the way the kitchen used to be before my aunt renovated it five years ago.

I collapse. Before I hit the floor, an arm catches me. The distinctive scent of aftershave draws my attention upward. A familiar man is holding me. He's in his late forties. His face is lined and he has more gray hair than before but there is no mistaking him. I pass out, looking into the concerned eyes of my father.

* * *

I hear the familiar roar and beeps of machines keeping me alive. An oxygen mask is tightly secured over the lower part of my face and needles connected to intravenous tubes protrude from my wrists. I manage to open my heavy eyelids enough to squint and take in the room.

Beside me sits my dad and a woman. Even though my eyes are barely open and the woman has aged, I recognize her instantly.

"Mom?"

I don't know if she can hear my whisper through the oxygen mask. I can hardly hear myself.

"Sweetie!" she says. "We're here."

My limited vision is blurred by tears. Mom lays her hand on my arm.

"It will all be okay. You just rest."

I don't say anything. I just stare at the two people I have longed to see again since the age of five. However, these aren't the parents who raised me until I was five. Clearly, something is amiss. I'm not in my world and might never see my aunt again. Still, I can't remember the last time I felt this whole.

My heavy eyelids close. Usually when in a hospital fighting for my life, my wish is that it's all a bad dream, and that I'll wake up in my bedroom at home. This time I hope that when I wake up, I will still be in this hospital bed.

This wish becomes reality. When my eyes open again, I can feel a tube under my nose and soreness in my wrist from the intravenous needle. The oxygen mask is gone. A doctor or nurse must have taken it off.

My parents are standing by the window. In my dad's former seat sits a familiar face—Dr. Freeman, one of the many specialists I've seen over the years. He looks just like the doctor I am used to seeing at home—a tall, thin man with sparse white hair and stubble.

We must be in some alternate reality where my parents never vanished. Therefore, as similar as Dr. Freeman may be to the doctor from home, this must be another version of him. That makes me consider a scary possibility when the doctor begins to speak.

"Hi, Synthia. I was just talking to your parents about your condition."

"Okay."

"Your CF symptoms have worsened. Why, I can't say. In addition, you have bronchitis again. We can treat you and in two to three weeks you should be mostly over it. But you'll need to stay here for at least a week, possibly two, for observation and treatment. Can you answer some questions?"

I nod.

"Have you been taking all of your medication this past week?"

"Of course," I lie, not ready to explain my situation to him or my parents. They wouldn't believe me anyway.

"And what about your treatments? Have you been wearing your physical therapy vest?"

"Of course she has," my mom answers. "She was wearing it before school this morning."

Damn. This is what I was afraid of.

"Have you been exercising and eating well?"

I just nod while trying to think about what to do next.

The doctor sighs. "All right. We're going to do more tests to figure out what caused this relapse."

"Thank you, Dr. Freeman," my father says. "We know she's in good hands."

Dr. Freeman exits the room and my parents leave me to rest. I lie there thinking about what to tell them. I'm in no shape to leave the hospital and run off so there's no escaping this.

An orderly brings dinner. He removes the top lid of the plastic tray and clicks it in place underneath. Roast beef and mashed potatoes, chicken broccoli soup with soda crackers, and a bun with a small container of cold, hard butter. And of course, no hospital meal would be complete without a cup of Jell-O. I'm not hungry but being in a world that doesn't prevent my illness, I need to get some calories into my system.

My mom comes in as I'm slurping up the last spoonful of soup. It's surreal seeing her in person. She's on the phone and is looking at me with bewilderment.

"I'm with my daughter right now. Tell me who this is or I'm hanging up."

My heart feels like it has dropped into my gut. This is what I feared would happen. I know who is on the other end of the phone. It's me.

Chapter 28

Talking to Myself

THERE IS A MIXTURE OF anger and confusion in my mom's eyes. "I wouldn't find this humorous under normal circumstances, but my daughter is in the hospital right now. This is not even remotely funny."

"Wait!" I say. "That's not a prank call. I'm—" It hurts to say it. "I'm...not actually your daughter."

"What are you talking about, Sweetheart?"

I motion for her to hand me the phone and she does.

"Syn?" I ask.

"Who is this?" the voice on the other end asks through tears and sniffles.

"I'm, uh, a friend," I tell her. "Come to the hospital." I glance at the number on the door. "Room 260B. I'll explain everything. It will all be okay."

"Who is this?" the other Syn asks again, desperate for an answer.

"See you soon." I hang up the phone and hand it to my mother.

She stares at me, completely perplexed. My dad walks in with a smile but when he observes her confusion, he becomes concerned.

"What's wrong? Is everything all right? Do you need anything?"

There is deep love for me in my dad's eyes. I wish he really was my dad. "Let me tell you the truth," I say.

My mom is less skeptical than my father because she had just talked to her daughter moments ago. As I tell them the truth, that I am from an alternate reality, I see the love they thought they had for me diminish. It's replaced with apprehension, confusion, and then anger.

"You impersonated our daughter?!" my mom says with venom in her voice. "How could you?!"

"I didn't—"

"You weren't even going to tell us, were you?" my dad asks. "Just get the medical care you need and leave. What do you think would happen to our Syn once you've altered her medical history?"

After all these years of dreaming about meeting my parents again, I'm crushed. What else was I supposed to do? I was dying when they found me. I might not technically be their daughter but I am still exactly like their child, and am suffering from the same disease.

Once they get the anger out of their systems, my mom asks how I got here. I tell her all about the Garden. This intrigues them.

They look at each other, like they're thinking the same thing.

"I don't expect you to believe me, but it's the truth."

"I believe you," my dad says. "A colleague of ours has been studying the multiverse for some time. She's been trying to determine a way to travel between different realities. My wife and I know that the science is there for healing properties in a small test environment."

"We've been working on that, trying to perfect it," my mom says, "but without success."

"We'll make sure you get the medical help you need," my dad says. "I would like to ask you for something in return."

"What's that?"

"Take us to this Garden. So our Syn can live her life without illness. Can you do that?"

"I'm not sure I can find my way back. But if I can, I'd be happy to take you all with me."

My mom rests her hand on mine and it feels so…right. "Thank you, Sweetie." She kisses my forehead.

"We'll let you rest," my dad says.

I'm tired and shut my eyes, trying to get as comfortable as possible while lying on my back, plugged into machines.

* * *

I don't know how long I slept. I cough a couple of times, open my eyes and gasp. There's a girl sitting in a chair beside me. It's me. The me from this reality. She gives me a wary smile.

Neither of us speaks. We just stare at each other in awe. She is physically identical to me in every way. Even her hair is cut the same way and she's dressed in black leggings and a loose-fitting blue tunic, clothes I would wear. We continue to analyze each part of our faces, searching for the slightest difference, but see nothing. I decide to break the ice.

"Hi," we both say in unison, like our minds are one.

We both laugh. I can see she's waiting to speak so that we don't do it again, at the same time.

I jump in. "Hi."

"Hi," she nervously replies. "This is so unreal."

"I have seen some pretty crazy things over the last week but still, I can hardly believe that I'm talking to...myself."

"How are you feeling?" she asks with genuine concern.

"Better. Still far from perfect but it doesn't feel like I'm going to die any more. At least not today." There is sorrow in her eyes at the mention of death and surely it's in mine as well.

"My parents told me you grew up as an orphan," she says after some thought.

"My parents went missing when I was five. I don't know if they're alive or not."

"I'm sorry," she says. "I can't imagine dealing with...everything...without them."

"It's been tough. But life isn't easy."

"No, it's not. My parents tell me it might get better. That you discovered a place where we can live without being sick. Is that really true?"

"It is. It's not like this world though. There are no cities. No TV or internet. The people live in log cabins. There are strange things there...in the Garden...things I don't understand. It is beautiful though."

"And we won't be sick in this...Garden?" the other Syn says, hopeful.

"That's right. Don't get your hopes up too high. I can't promise that I can find a way back."

"But you'll try?"

"Of course."

My other self leans in like she's about to hug me, then flinches, as if thinking about how weird that would be. We simply stare at each other in amazement. After a few minutes, my parents come in.

"How are you two doing?" my dad asks as he walks over to the other Syn and gives her a kiss. It's evident who their love gravitates toward and although disappointed, I do understand. She is their daughter and to them I'm the equivalent of a clone.

"Syn," my father says to his daughter, "you should head home. I asked the staff to leave us alone for a while, but someone will come in soon and explaining why there are two of you could be challenging."

"I understand." She stands up and looks my way. "So glad to meet you."

"Me too," I say with a smile. "See you soon."

The other Syn nods and takes one last long look at me before leaving the room.

My dad sits down in the chair next to my bed. "The doctors think you should spend at least a week here to play it safe. Then we'll take you to our place and try to find a way back to the Garden. I've talked to our research partner and she said she'll help us."

"Masie Winters?"

"Yes," my dad confirms, eyeing me with suspicion. "How did you know that?"

"She worked with my parents before they disappeared." I refrain from telling him that she disappeared along with my parents or that the police found her charred body. I don't know what that would accomplish.

"Yes, of course."

The nurse comes in to check on me and my parents exit. I've been hospitalized for bronchitis more times than I can count. Recovery mostly involves a lot of rest, but in addition to my regular treatments, they'll give me anti-inflammatory drugs. They'll take lung x-rays, and blood and urine tests to make sure the infection doesn't turn into anything worse, and so the doctor can try to find out why my CF symptoms have worsened. I'll also continue all my regular treatments that I would normally do at home.

My parents don't spend much time with me over the next two days. When I ask to see their Syn, they tell me we will meet again soon. It seems like they're brushing me off. Something doesn't feel right.

On the third day, I don't see anyone except for the doctors, nurses, and orderlies. I begin to worry that they have found the entrance to the Garden and went there without me. Would they actually do that and leave me here?

By the third night, I'm feeling a lot better. Four hours into a solid sleep, I feel a hand shaking my shoulder. The overhead light is off but it's not too dark because of the light coming from the medical equipment and the hallway. I adjust my eyes and see the young girl from the Garden who saved me from the reptile dogs.

"I had trouble finding you," she tells me. "Are you okay?"

"I'm doing better. What are you doing here?"

"I'm here to take you back to the Garden. The lightway only stays open for so long."

"The lightway?"

"The portals that take you from one world to another. The longer you stay here, the chance the portal will permanently close before you reach it increases. Are you healthy enough to get out of here?"

"I feel okay. If I go too long without treatments though, I could relapse."

"Go to sleep and we'll go first thing in the morning."

"I promised my parents—my parents from this world—and the other me that I'll take them with me."

"I know," the girl says and stares me down. "And I'm sorry…they can't come with us."

Chapter 29

Point Blank

I TELL THE GIRL THAT I'm not leaving without them. That I need to keep my promise. Her eyes are sympathetic as she explains the situation.

"There are three types of lightways," she begins. "There are lightways that are open to anyone who enters. Like the one you came through from your own world. Those lightways are purposefully placed by someone and they go directly to the Garden you entered and back again, but not to any other realities."

This means someone placed the portal in my pond on purpose. I remember how I was pushed into the water. Someone *wanted* me to go to the Garden. Why? And if it takes you back again, why wasn't it in the pond when I swam down there?

"Then there are the lightways that open up in the fog," the girl continues. "There's no telling where those portals will take you. You don't know until you enter the light."

"If you don't know where it will take you, how did you find your way here?" I ask.

"That's a good question," she says with a mysterious smile. "The last type of lightway portal opens up in whichever world you have reached when you enter a lightway in the fog," she continues without answering my question. "Like the world we're in right now. It opens somewhere close to where you arrived and only stays open for a little while. The time varies. Usually at least a week or a bit longer. Sometimes it only stays open for a few days. That's why we need to leave soon."

"It will take us back to the Garden?"

"Possibly. Or it may take us to another world. This type of lightway will appear only to those who arrived through another portal."

"You mean—"

"Yes. It won't appear—or even exist—to the other you or her parents. Before I came here, I saw them looking for it."

"Without me?" I ask, disappointed.

"Without you. Not that they will find it. They can't."

I feel for the other Syn. I got her hopes up about living a life without illness. Now they are going to be dashed.

"Get some sleep," the girl says. "I'll take you to the portal in the morning."

"Thank you. What's your name?"

"Beth."

As I close my eyes, I picture Beth's face. She doesn't look exactly like I did at her age. Her eyes are darker, her eyebrows thicker. I think I've figured out who she is and the thought comforts me as I fall asleep.

When my eyes open in the morning, I expect to see Beth sitting next to me. Instead, a nurse is standing over me, adjusting the oxygen tank.

"Good morning," she says.

"Was there a girl just here?"

"A girl? No, only you."

An orderly enters carrying a tray with a pile of scrambled eggs, diced hash browns, two English muffins—with small packets of strawberry jam and peanut butter—two bananas, yogurt, and a couple of enzyme pills.

When I'm done eating, I'm given a bunch more pills to take. Some are not what I'm used to taking. The other Syn must have been prescribed different medication. I'm scared to take pills my body isn't used to, and save the unfamiliar pills for last, stashing them in my cheek until the nurse leaves. When she's gone, I spit them into a piece of tissue and stuff it under the mattress. Hopefully I'll be long gone by the time someone notices.

I spend almost half an hour in a vibrating physical therapy vest. Its familiar presence feels oddly reassuring as it shakes my lungs. Less than a minute after the nurse leaves me to rest, Beth walks in.

"Have you finished your treatments? How do you feel?"

I nod. "I feel pretty good, considering."

"Are you strong enough to go?"

"I think so. Once we get to the Garden, I'll be as good as new."

"Oh," Beth says, "that's not how it works. Remember, the lightways that appear in new worlds don't always go directly to the Garden. More times than not, they don't. You have to travel through three to eight worlds, possibly more, before you get back."

"Why?" I ask, confused.

"I have no idea," Beth admits. "That's just the way it is. Unless there are obstacles in our way— and usually there aren't—it shouldn't take more than an hour or two to return to the Garden after we enter the first lightway."

"Okay." I rip off my sheets and blanket. As my feet dangle over the side of the bed I start to cough up mucus caught in my throat. The coughing goes on for almost a minute, while Beth watches, extremely concerned.

"Let's get out of here," I rasp weakly as the coughing dwindles.

Beth tosses over my clothes and waits outside while I change. Once we have snuck out of the hospital, she motions me toward a green taxicab.

"It's been waiting for us. The driver knows the address."

She's pretty mature for someone who's barely ten years old. The taxi drives down Broadway, Redfern's main street. Although most of the city streets look the same as they do at home in my real world, some storefronts are different. A small corner in a mini-mall that is a KFC at home is a UPS store here. A four-floor apartment building stands here where a car wash is in my world. Something must have happened for things to occur differently. I wonder what happened in this world so that my parents didn't disappear.

We pass my school. It looks the same as far as I can tell.

I cough up more phlegm and spit it into a tissue.

"Are you okay?" Beth asks.

The driver is watching in the rear-view mirror.

"I'm fine." The truth is I'm tired and my chest feels heavy.

Rather than stopping in front of my house (or at least this world's version of my house), we stop a block away in front of the exotic animal sanctuary. Beth pulls out a wad of cash and counts out thirty dollars for the fare.

There must be hundreds of dollars in that wad! Where did she get it all? The meter reads $19.85 but Beth hands the driver a twenty and a ten and tells him to keep the change. He beams and thanks us as we exit the cab.

The taxi drives away. Someone is calling my name. Across the street, Joel Anderson is on his knees changing a tire.

I return his greeting and we move on. He thinks I'm the other Syn and I don't want to get into a conversation. We finally arrive at my house and when I turn right to head to the driveway, Beth tugs on my sleeve.

"This way." She pulls me in the direction of the Sanders' farm. We walk down the driveway, past their house, toward their acreage of blueberry bushes. A loud click sounds behind us and we freeze for a split second.

"Turn around!"

Beth and I spin around to see my mom and dad standing on the Sanders' driveway. My dad is holding a rifle and it's aimed directly at me.

Chapter 30

Syns of the Father

"STAY WHERE YOU ARE!" my dad shouts. He tilts his head in my mom's direction. "Get Syn," he tells her, referring of course to my other.

My mom runs back to the house. I start to shiver. My own father, holding a gun on me. I may not be his actual daughter but I look, sound, and think just like her.

"You're going to take us to the Garden," he orders.

"You don't need to hold us at gunpoint," I say.

"I can't take any chances."

My mom comes out of the house with the other Syn following.

"What are you doing, Dad?!" the other Syn shouts.

"Don't worry."

The other Syn runs up to him. "Dad, put the gun down!" She glances my way shamefully.

"Take us to the portal," my dad says, ignoring her.

I am about to tell him that we can't take them but Beth speaks first.

"Okay, we'll take you." She points past my dad to the side of the house. "It's in your garden."

"We scoured the entire area," he says. "We didn't see anything."

"You don't know what to look for," Beth says. She doesn't seem at all rattled. I admire the bravery of such a young girl.

"All right," he says. "Lead the way."

I follow Beth down the driveway and past the carport, my parents and the other Syn following close behind.

"Put the gun down, Dad," the other Syn pleads again. "I trust her. She's just like me."

"Your life is at stake!" he argues.

As we walk through the garden the other Syn begins to cry, which causes her to cough and snort. I feel badly for her, even though she has had the life I've wished for so many times. We're walking around the pond. The tip of the rifle juts into my back.

"How much farther?" he asks. "Where the hell is this thing!"

Despite having a rifle jammed against my back, fury rages inside of me rather than fear. I spin around and face him. The rifle rams into the center of my chest.

"How can you point a gun at me? I'm your daughter!"

"Like hell you are!"

Tears blur my vision. I force myself to stay calm so I don't end up with a phlegm attack.

"Just show us the portal," my mom says. "That's all we want."

"Dad, leave her alone!" the other Syn yells. "She wants to help us."

The rifle is still pressing against my shirt. "I always wished that I grew up with my parents. But if they're anything like you, I hope they're dead!"

My dad flips the rifle around and bangs me in the forehead with its butt, knocking me to the grass and sending me into a coughing frenzy. Then he points the rifle at Beth. "Tell me where this damn portal is or I'll shoot you both. Her first."

And then the other Syn does what I imagine I would do if our roles were reversed. She pulls herself away from her mother and shoves her father. Caught by surprise, he trips and falls into the pond.

I only look at my other for a second but it feels like we share a long moment.

Beth grabs my hand. "Run!"

And run we do. I follow Beth past the pond and past the tree where my parents' initials are carved. We run all the way to the fence at the back of my family's property, pausing at the sound of a gunshot. I look back. There is nobody in sight but we can hear my dad's footsteps.

Something catches my eye. A narrow stream of white light is shooting out of a dandelion that's growing against a fence post. Beth bends down and rips out the dandelion and the stream of light shoots up. It shines like a spotlight. She leaps into the light and tugs my arm, drawing me beside her.

Time seems to slow like before. My father is running in slow motion with the rifle aimed right at us. There is a loud bang and smoke flares from the barrel. The bullet speeds toward us as we're surrounded by white light. Just before the bullet is about to hit me, I'm engulfed by the light and moments later, my body crash-lands on soft ground.

Beth has disappeared. There's nothing to do except see where the light has taken me. The white light dissipates. I'm in the exact same spot in the Garden that I was just in with Beth. But my dad is no longer there and the grass is taller and dried up. I look around again, and there is Beth.

I'm in shock. Tears are flowing down my cheeks, yet Beth is calm and composed.

"Where are we?"

"In another world," Beth says.

"He shot at us!" I exclaim. "At *me*. His own daughter!"

"I'm sorry you had to see that. I should have warned you."

"Warned me about what?"

"I've traveled to so many worlds. Sometimes they're just a little different, and sometimes the changes are extreme. The few times I met your parents they were always pretty much like how they were just now. They weren't the people I knew."

Beth puts on a brave face although she's suppressing tears of her own.

"Beth, they're your parents too, aren't they?"

Beth nods and her tears spill. I step toward her and embrace my sister.

* * *

Beth and I scour every inch of the Garden, starting from the back fence. She says that the lightway could be on a neighboring property but we decide to check this one first. A lawnmower is roaring at the front of the garden and I hope to hell it's not a version of my father pushing it. I don't think I can deal with that again so soon.

As we search for the portal, Beth tells me that our mother gave birth to her in the Garden and our parents raised her there until she was six. They were kind and loving, unlike the other versions she has met. They spent a lot of time working on their equipment but Beth didn't know exactly what they were working on. They lived in harmony with the others in the Garden, including the Creepers.

Then one day they were gone and an older girl was living in their house. She stayed in the shadows and never let anyone see her face. The girl let Beth live in the Garden so long as she stayed away from the house. Beth tells me how she's lived much of her life in other realities. She felt trapped in the Garden though, and has spent years exploring other versions of the world, never staying more than a couple of days in one place—just long enough to learn from their books, their TVs, and their internet.

"The girl who stayed in the shadows, that's Sinister, right?" I ask. "The woman who claims to be the queen of the Garden?"

Beth nods. "I overheard her planning something bad. Something to do with you."

"What?"

"I don't know. But I'm *sure* it's bad. And—"

"Hi there."

We're interrupted by a deep voice. I look up at an older teenage boy with olive skin. He's wearing ripped, beige shorts and a white tank top that shows off his muscular body. And his face—there's no mistaking it. It's like the Latino part of Cole.

"Cole?"

"Cole? No, my name's Darren."

"Darren?" I repeat, confused. "What are you doing here?"

"I work here. I'm a gardener."

"You work for the Wade family?"

Beth bites her lip. "Syn…"

"The Wade family?" Darren asks, puzzled. "Aren't they the ones who used to live here? Before—"

"Syn," Beth interrupts. "Let's go."

"I want to hear what he says! Before what?"

"Before they were all killed."

"Syn…" Beth pleads.

"Killed?"

"Well, murdered," Darren says.

Beth tugs my sleeve. I ignore her.

"Murdered?!"

"The parents and the sick daughter. Everyone around here knows about that."

My heart sinks. Not just because this version of my family, including me was killed, but because I can tell that the "everyone" who knows about the murders includes my own sister.

Chapter 31

The End of the World

"COME TO THINK OF it, you look a lot like the girl who was killed," Darren says.

I glance at Beth without uttering a word, then walk past Darren to the house. Beth follows.

"Man, I'm sorry," I hear Darren say. "That wasn't cool."

I turn around to see his familiar face one more time. "Don't worry about it."

"You knew," I say to Beth as we stroll to the house. "I could see it on your face. How did you know my—our—family was killed in this world?"

"I didn't know. I just wasn't surprised. I've traveled through a lot of different worlds. In more than a few of them, you and our parents were killed. Once I even walked in and found them all…you know. Like it happened just before I got there. It was horrible."

First I learn most versions of my parents aren't the good-hearted people who raised me and now, that they—and me—are being repeatedly targeted and murdered? It's so much to take in.

"Why would someone want to kill us, Beth?"

"I don't know."

"Have you ever been in worlds where I'm living with my Aunt Ruth?"

"A few times."

"And…"

"You were alive. Your aunt too."

"So maybe the motive for killing me only exists in a reality where my parents are alive."

"Maybe."

Suddenly, Beth's eyes widen and she points toward the carport. "There!"

A dirty red pickup is parked in the carport. Its front seats are glowing white. We rush over. It's unlocked. I open the door and leap in. As the light embraces me, I see Beth yell something with a panicked look on her face. In slow motion, she runs to the other side of the truck. Before she can get in, I'm fully embraced by the white light.

When the light dissipates, something is pricking my legs and behind. The air is extremely hot and humid. I'm sitting on a pile of broken pieces of wood and concrete rubble. Surrounding me is widespread wreckage, like in the wake of a massive hurricane. There isn't a plant or blade of grass in sight. There is also no sign of life except for me. No birds, no bugs, and certainly no other humans.

It seems Beth may have been stranded in that other world when I entered the lightway before her. God, I hope not. I decide to wait a bit in the hope that she'll arrive soon.

Heavy waves of heat beat against my skin. Surprisingly, the sky isn't clear blue like one would expect it to be on a hot, sunny day. Instead, the sky is covered with thick red fog. Or, smog. Why is it red? Why is this place nothing but a dried-up wasteland? Could this be the aftermath of a nuclear war? That could explain why I don't see a single sign of life.

As I ponder this horrible thought, congestion starts building in my chest. I cough repeatedly for at least a minute, yet the soreness in my chest remains. This must be lingering effects from the bronchitis, not to mention the fact that I didn't take all the meds in the hospital or complete all of my treatments. I need to get to the Garden soon.

I hack away, while gazing around curiously. Somewhere nearby is a lightway but with so many pieces of broken wood, concrete, and metal shards, it's hard to know where to begin looking. Since I traveled here from the carport that is likely where the lightway dropped me in this new world. I take a closer look at the debris and make a mental note of a chipped red brick leaning against a large piece of broken concrete. Then I walk to where my house would have been and look closely at the debris on the ground, searching the area that should be the front yard. False hope is raised when something shines in my face a couple of times. In both cases, it was just the sun reflecting off a piece of metal or broken glass.

Phlegm continues to build up in my chest and uncontrollable hacking takes over. The fit finally passes, leaving fresh blood splattered on my shirt, and on my legs and feet. When I cough up blood at home, Aunt Ruth takes me to the hospital right away. I need to get to a hospital or find the Garden soon, or else I'm in big trouble.

The coughing is ongoing as I scour the area. More phlegm and spatters of blood. I desperately need water and can't imagine where to look for it. Every minute, my symptoms worsen. I'll die in this hellish world unless I find the lightway, and *soon*.

Twenty minutes later I have scoured the entire property. Could the lightway be farther away? Is the object the lightway's attached to buried under all this rubble? I have no idea. I decide to return to where my search began and start again. Maybe while coughing, my eyes missed something.

After locating the chipped red brick, I endure another coughing fit. My already grubby hands are splattered with blood. I need to hurry! Fighting increasing weakness, I force myself to sweep through the rubble a second time. The second extensive search reveals nothing. While catching my breath, I glance around, wondering if there ever was a pond here. A few steps later, I find out after treading on what looks like firm clay. The surface crumbles, dropping me several feet down.

Surfacing before me is a graveyard of bones—thousands of them. Skeletons, some human and some from mammals. Few are intact. A few inches in front of my face is part of what looks like a rat or mouse skeleton. Why so many skeletons in this particular place? After whatever destroyed this world, were there survivors who threw these bones in the now dried-up pond?

I can't waste precious time thinking about this. I shakily rise to my feet, leaning forward, coughing again. More blood. Now, gasping and retching from intense pain in my chest. I breathlessly cry for help but unless Beth has found a way to follow me, my pleas will likely go unheard. I lie back, succumbing to pain and exhaustion.

* * *

When I open my eyes, it's nighttime. There are no stars and the only light is from the moon, though its placement in the sky is a mystery. The atmosphere is still very warm and humid and my throat throbs with every breath. I cough a couple of times and try to push myself up. Too weak. No strength to yell. If Beth is out there, she will have to find me on her own. My tiny glimmer of hope rests solely on her rescuing me again.

I lie motionless on an uncomfortable bed of bones, wishing that Beth had been part of my life growing up. Having a sister would have been wonderful. My thoughts turn to Aunt Ruth, who devoted her life to me without much recognition. She will never know what happened to me. I think of Janna, reluctantly accepting that she must be gone by now. I'm not religious and have always believed that once you die, you're just gone, and now, can't help but wonder if—hope—that I will see my dear friend once again after I'm gone. Falling back into a slumber, I wonder if my parents are alive somewhere, and wish I had found out why they came to the Garden, and where they disappeared to afterward.

After waiting for what seems like hours, my hopes that Beth will arrive have dwindled. I'm truly afraid I'll die here, alone, in this wasteland of bones. And then I see the light.

Chapter 32

A Grim Revelation

A GLIMMER OF LIGHT. A glimmer of hope. Twenty, maybe thirty feet away, is a dim glow. It's escaping from something at the bottom of the dry pond.

It feels like I'm about to die. Yet, the possibility of living on gives me enough of an energy boost to crawl, digging my hands into the boney dirt and dragging my body barely one inch. Then another inch. My mouth is so dry I can barely stretch my lips apart to gasp for air. Miraculously, I manage to pull myself to the origin of the glow and brush the dirt off of it. The glowing object is a skeleton.

While heaving myself up alongside the shining object, I realize that the skeleton is the exact length of my body. There isn't much time to think about that though. The light quickly expands and I'm encompassed by the glow.

When the light dissipates, I find myself engulfed in water and instinctively open my mouth, choking as it rushes in. I've escaped a post-apocalyptic world, only to drown in another world. Convinced that I'm drowning, flailing arms clutching at a wall of clay, I feel no symptoms of my illness! It's safe to assume that the light has landed me in the Garden's pond again.

I look up, trying to dog paddle with the little strength that is left, and am startled by a hand reaching into the water. In desperation, I raise an arm and the hand grabs my wrist. With one great tug, my head is lifted out of the water. Water gurgles from my mouth, spewing forth, emptying from my lungs. I'm lying on the grass now. Sweet, blessed oxygen. I'm grateful to see Wolf leaning over me.

"Don't you think it's a bit late for a swim?" he says and smiles. He bends down and covers me with a heavy blanket.

"Thank you," I gasp through chattering teeth as cool air encircles my soaking wet body. I try to catch my breath. "What are you doing out here so late?"

"Sometimes when the sky is clear and the moon is this bright, I like to sleep under the stars."

"Lucky for me."

"Syn? What are you doing out here? I wasn't sleeping and didn't see you jump in."

"It's complicated." I stand up and hand Wolf the blanket. My strength has returned. "I need to go. Thank you again."

"Any time," Wolf says, scratching his head.

At Rose's cabin, I discreetly open the door and peek inside. Flint is sound asleep on the couch. I sneak past him and snatch a fresh change of clothes, and once outside, gently close the door with great relief. I'm getting some answers. Tonight!

I look around to make sure no one is there and quickly change into Lily's clothes. Then, head for Cole's cabin, hoping to count on him for some backup. I sneak through the orchard so Wolf won't see me.

Cole's cabin is dark. I rap on the door softly and wait, peering nervously into the shadows. No answer. I knock louder. Still nothing. Hardly daring to breathe, I grip the door handle and turn it bit by bit. The door swings open. I creep through the main room into his bedroom, which glows blue in the moonlight. His bed is empty and neatly made. Where could he be? Perhaps he's sleeping under the stars as well.

I open the fridge before leaving. There isn't too much in there except for a pitcher of water, a block of cheese, veggies, and raw fish wrapped in cellophane. I take the fish. Tomorrow, I'll tell Cole why. He'll understand.

Wolf is sleeping on his back as I tiptoe past the pond. Once I'm out of sight, I kneel down to open the plastic wrap. There are two fillets; exactly what I require. I tear the plastic with my teeth and wrap each fillet separately. In movies, guard dogs are often distracted by raw steak. I can only hope that Sinister's dogs like raw fish.

When I get to the end of the path, I take a deep breath before making my way to the carport. Walking quickly, trying not to look at the cemetery, I still feel dizzy. As usual, there are whispers in my head that are too scrambled to understand. By the time I reach the carport, the queasiness subsides. Good. Now, down the pathway to the front steps.

Climbing slowly, my gaze rests on the heavy, ominous double doors, which seem to stare at me. My knuckles have barely rapped on the door, and it opens. It's difficult to make out anything inside, except for that familiar dim blue glow. I had planned to confront Sinister in a semi-civilized manner, by knocking on her door and asking for answers. And yet, the door is open like she's waiting for me to let myself in. Resisting the bad feeling in the pit of my stomach, I go inside, dangling the fish from one hand.

The blue glow provides enough light for me to move through the room. I leave the door open in case I need to make a quick getaway. I'm about to yell hello when there is a creaking sound upstairs. As I approach the second floor, slowing at the top of the stairs, the fear is overwhelming.

It's darker up here. Light is shining from the master bedroom at the end of the hallway—the room that my aunt sleeps in and my parents before her. I hear another creak, which comes from the bedroom.

I walk toward the master bedroom, peeking through open doorways on the way. The rooms are filled with old-fashioned computer equipment. As I pass the bathroom, a floorboard squeaks under my foot. I freeze.

A voice calls from the master bedroom. "Baby, come to bed. It's late!"

That voice. I know that voice! The feeling of dread from before pales in comparison to this.

I take three more steps. The face of the person lying in bed matches the voice. The fish slides from my hand onto the floor and slips through the railing, falling to the main floor.

Cole is bare-chested, his eyes riveted on mine. At first he seems genuinely surprised to see me.

"Syn. I know what this looks like." Then the corners of his mouth twist upward into a deeply disturbing grin. "Okay, this is *exactly* what it looks like."

Chapter 33

Sleeping with the Enemy

COLE STANDS UP BESIDE THE bed, wearing nothing but boxer shorts. I turn and run to the stairs with him chasing me. He shoves me at the top of the staircase and I tumble down the first set of stairs. My head whacks the railing on the landing, bringing me to an abrupt stop.

Blood trickles from my head. But it's not the blood, or the pain, or even the sound of Cole's feet thumping down the stairs that chills me to the bone. The feeling of Cole's hand pushing me was exactly like when I was pushed into the pond in my garden at home!

Holding one hand over my bleeding forehead, I look up at Cole, who towers over me. "It was you. You brought me here."

Cole glares down at me. He grabs my hair, yanks my head up, and smashes my face against the hardwood floor.

* * *

I'm awakened by someone slapping my cheek. Blood has crusted on my face below my nose. I'm sitting in a chair with my arms tied behind me. My legs are strapped to the front of the chair, which sits next to the glowing blue dome, facing the long length of the main floor of the house. My nose is throbbing. If Cole broke it, it's already healing itself.

Cole is standing over me. He leans down and once kind eyes stare into mine. This is not the same Cole from the Garden, who befriended me and won my heart. I'm deathly afraid that the Cole I thought I knew was a fabrication from the moment we met. If the situation were different, I might laugh at the irony that the boy who literally has two faces has turned out to be two-faced.

"Wake up, Sunshine," Cole says, in a mockingly cheerful tone. "I want to introduce you to someone."

I stare into his narrowed eyes, full of contempt for the guy I thought I knew. "What's wrong with you?"

Cole fakes a look of confusion. "Oh, no. You didn't fall for me, did you? I hope I didn't give you the wrong impression. You're a nice girl and all, but my heart belongs to someone else."

He gestures gracefully to present the person I know only as Sinister. She is sitting in a chair four to five feet in front of the stairs that lead to the basement. Beth described her as a girl, yet she's at least my age. She is wearing a dark robe with a hood that shadows her eyes, and that metal mask covers the rest of her face. Sitting on each side of her are her two pet Creepers, their snouts raised, sniffing the air. They smell the fish and turn away from Sinister to follow the blessed scent.

"Sit!" she screams.

They lick their lips nervously and promptly sit. Sinister stands up and moves closer. "Synthia Wade," she says in a loud, raspy whisper. "We finally meet on my terms."

"Sinister." My tone is icy.

"I really don't like how that name stuck, but what can I expect after living in the shadows for so long? Why don't you just call me Sin for short?"

I don't even blink in response to her wry smile.

"I knew your little guardian angel would keep you safe and in one piece," Sinister says. "She's a tad predictable."

"What do you want from me? Why did Cole bring me to the Garden?"

"Those are two very good questions." Sinister tilts her head in Cole's direction. "Coleus, would you be so kind as to prepare the equipment downstairs while I try my best to quench the curiosity of our dear guest?"

"I'd be happy to, my love," he says, beaming at her on his way to the stairs.

If my hands were free, I'd clobber myself for having been so stupid. "What do you want from me?" I ask again.

"Everything you have! Oh wait, I'm getting ahead of myself. You have a lot of questions. While Coleus is setting up, I'll tell you a little story that should help clarify my intentions."

I strain against the tight ropes, trying to loosen them without revealing the effort on my face.

"Once upon a time, there was a little girl named Synthia. Syn for short. This girl had two scientists for parents. They loved her more than anything else in the universe. When Syn was diagnosed with a disease that would one day cut her life short, they went to great lengths to find a cure for their beloved daughter."

My parents tried to find a cure? This is news to me. I do remember them spending extended periods of time in their basement lab or on trips. Perhaps that's what they were doing?

"Unfortunately," Sinister goes on, "these devoted parents didn't have the know-how to create a cure. Researchers had been trying for years without success. What they believed they could do, however, was cure their daughter of *all* illness. Essentially, with a fountain of youth that would correct any irregularities in her body and allow her to live forever.

"As with all scientific experiments, it was a long process. The girl's parents believed they could create an environment where subjects were immune to illness. Their hope was to transfer the healing properties of that place to their daughter. But they needed a test environment—and test subjects, of course."

"Are you saying my parents created this place as an alternate world, to try and cure me?"

"In a matter of speaking," Sinister says, abandoning her pretense of telling a story. "Their research partner Masie Winters had recently made a breakthrough that allowed her to enter parallel worlds. You see, Ms. Winters confirmed what many scientists had believed for years. The existence of a multiverse. An infinite number of parallel realities, with new ones created every moment. Each new world is born as a result of one single action in another world. It may be something as minuscule as a boy sneezing once in one world and twice in the new one. Such a tiny event could create a nearly identical new world or have a butterfly effect that could ultimately end human existence."

I think of the lifeless world I nearly died in before returning to the Garden.

"And in each new world, further worlds would continue to pop up. No one has had absolute proof of this until recently. Ms. Winters, however, not only created a way to visit these alternate worlds, but her colleagues Ian and Debra Wade believed that based on her research, they could create a reality where they could do their own experiments."

Cole stomps up the stairs, drops a large metal box with several cords hanging from it onto the floor, and returns to the dark stairway. He gives me a smirk before descending again. "Don't mind me."

"Your parents approached Masie Winters about using her research to help create this new reality to help their daughter. I don't know if it was a matter of pride or if she was morally against the prospect of playing God, but she refused their request. Your parents, however, were determined to save their daughter's life and so without Masie Winters' knowledge, they used her scientific findings to create a new world."

"My parents wouldn't steal their partner's work. They weren't like that!" I protest, doubting my own words. Perhaps if they were determined to save my life, they might have resorted to doing things they wouldn't have done otherwise.

"Stealing Winters' work was the least of your parents' sins. Would you like to know about all the blood on their hands? The torture? The deaths?"

"You're crazy!" I scream, squirming against the ropes, making good use of this distraction to loosen them. How can I believe anything she says when she's making these insane accusations?

Sinister comes closer. Her Creeper companions do the same. "I'm not crazy. Your parents created the world you're in right now. They ripped portions of land from alternate worlds to build this one. The people and other creatures in the Garden were also ripped from their worlds, all memories of former lives erased. You visited the underground society. The creatures down there, like my loyal companions beside me, were unintentionally combined from multiple lives. I'll let Coleus fill your innocent mind with images of the devastations they caused."

The ropes are as tight as ever. I don't believe a word of what she's told me, though I have to admit she seems to believe the garbage she's spewing.

"This Garden shares the sky with another world. The day your parents created this world, they spent hours experimenting with portions of upper atmospheres from other worlds to find an ideal weather system. The constant fluctuations disoriented pilots and brought their planes crashing down into this world. More than a thousand passengers' lives were lost because of your parents' selfishness."

Her story matches Rose's. An icy chill runs down my spine. Could what she's saying actually be true?

"That was just the beginning. Your parents needed test subjects. Sick people who would benefit from the healing atmosphere they created. They wanted to transfer the healing elements to the test subjects so they could survive outside of the Garden. Using Winters' research, they created a bubble world…a blank reality. A white nothing. They would inflict test subjects with horrible illnesses—cancer, AIDS, and leprosy, to name a few—and isolate them in the bubble so they could attempt to transfer the Garden's healing energy to them. Each time they failed, they put on hazmat suits and poked, prodded, cut, and tore into those innocent people to see what went wrong."

"You're lying!" My wrists are burning from twisting against the ropes.

Sinister moves closer. Even though her face is covered with a mask, I can see the intensity of the anger in her eyes through the holes.

"I am telling the truth," she says evenly. "But you haven't heard the most horrifying part yet. You see, *Synthia*, your parents couldn't have just any test subjects. They needed ones with your genetic makeup. Because they weren't trying to cure the world of disease. Just you."

The anticipated truth is searing through my gut. I'm terrified to hear anymore. Can't cover my ears. *Damn these ropes!*

"The dozens of test subjects they infected with disease, then cut up like lab rats and buried in the dirt had a lot in common with you. In fact, they *were* you."

I can't look away from her paralyzing presence.

"They *were* you," she repeats with a sneer. "In different realities, different versions of you lived similar lives. Sick, but part of a loving family and with a lust for life. Your parents tore them from their lives. Away from their parents, who were nearly identical to themselves by the way, leaving them with unanswered questions about the loss of their daughters. They were so cold and heartless they didn't even consider the pain of their other selves."

"I don't believe you!"

"Don't you?" Sinister is gloating now. "I know you've seen the cemetery outside this house. Who do you think is buried in those graves?"

"You're lying!"

"Oh, but you've heard those whispers. You've heard them enter your mind. To try and communicate with you. Those are the voices of your others. When your parents were done with them, they took them up the stairway to the clouds, where they were technically in the skies of another world without healing properties, and killed them there. Because their bodies were buried in the Garden, the essence of their spirits remains here. You can hear them because you share their soul. The souls of dozens of young Synthia Wades, who were ripped from their homes, mutilated and murdered, all so maybe, just *maybe*, you could live."

"I don't believe you! I'll never believe you!" In my angst, I jerk the chair an inch closer to this monstrous liar.

Sin shoves her face into mine. "You *should* believe me! Because I have suffered the torture your parents inflicted on so many others!"

With her gloved hands, she grips each side of the metal mask and pries it off. The skin underneath sizzles and steam rises from her face. Once the steam evaporates, I see a teenage girl with skin that bubbles like a pool of lava. Her injuries distort the features of her face, but looking into the girl's pupils, there's no mistaking whose eyes are staring back at me. My own.

Chapter 34

Original Syn

"You're one of them. One of…me," I mumble through my tears.

"That's right." She pulls off her hood. "The last test subject. The only survivor."

I now believe everything she has told me is true. The people in the Garden referred to her as Sinister, but in reality she was *Synister*, a sick play on words. A dark version of me, twisted from the torture my parents put her through.

"Your face…"

"Yes. Pretty hideous, isn't it? Your parents injected me with so many diseases that even with the Garden's healing properties my illnesses are always trying to break through. The cold mask soothes my burning skin and reduces some pain, though only a little."

"I—I'm sorry." My words surprise me.

"Oh no, you're not. Soon, you will be."

Cole thumps up the stairs and plunks two metal helmets on the floor. Several colored cords connect the helmets to each other. There is also one cord that exits one of the helmets with what looks like an IV needle attached to the end of it.

Cole smiles at me. "So the mask has come off. She won't look like that for long though, thanks to you."

"What is he talking about?"

"How much longer?" Synister asks Cole, ignoring me.

"Five minutes maybe, ten tops."

"Good. That should be enough time to tell our guest the rest of the story before we begin."

"Begin what?"

"You'll see. But for now, wouldn't you like to find out why your parents never came back all those years ago?"

Of course I do, but refuse to give her the satisfaction of answering.

"I know you do. Did you ever meet Masie Winters?"

"A couple of times. When I was young."

"I hear she was a calm, focused young woman. However, when she found out that your parents went behind her back and used her research to create a new world, she was furious at their betrayal. She transported your parents to the world they created and implemented a program to prevent them from exiting the Garden to return to their world."

"The night my parents disappeared…they said they were going to take me somewhere. Someplace special."

"When they discovered that Masie had found out what they were up to, they panicked and planned to bring you here, to live healthily and happily for the rest of existence. Masie trapped them before they had a chance to escape with you."

After all these years of wondering what happened, as horrible as this is, it's a relief to know the truth. "Where are they now?"

"Let me show you."

Synister strolls over to a monitor and hits the power button. And there they are! Sitting in a room of endless white nothingness. They look much older than my parents did in that alternate world. My dad's gray beard is long. Both of them are sitting quietly and still. They appear lost and defeated.

"Mom! Dad!"

"They can't hear you."

"Where are they? How did they get there?"

"They are where I spent years of my life. In the bubble."

"How—?"

"Even after they were trapped in the Garden they continued their experiments on me and other test subjects, just in case they managed to find a way back one day. I am the last surviving test subject. A few years ago, there was some sort of glitch—don't know what happened—that phased me out of the bubble and into this house. While your parents were on their computers frantically trying to fix whatever had gone wrong, I hid in a corner and let the Garden's properties heal me to the extent that they could. When your parents realized the bubble was empty, they phased themselves into it to look for me. While they were there, I pulled all the plugs, trapping them in their own prison. They've been there ever since."

Their skinny, pale bodies and hopeless faces are hard to look at. Even though they have done so many terrible things, I want to see them in person so badly.

"It took a few days," Synister went on, "but I figured out how to get in and out of the bubble. For ages, Coleus has been trying to convince me to kill your parents and though it's been very tempting, I've let them live in return for information about human genetics and how the lightways and all this technology works. If they don't cooperate, they starve."

"And Cole tells you what's happening in the Garden."

As if on cue, Cole climbs back up the basement stairs. "Those idiots think she's monitoring them with hidden cameras. But it's really just me, gaining their trust and reporting back to my love."

He passionately kisses her scabby lips, then smiles at me. "Jealous?"

"Not one bit."

He sneers and shuts off the monitor, my parents disappearing from my life once again. "Wait until you see what we're going to do to you."

"Do whatever you want with me. But let my parents go."

"Are you freakin' serious?!" Cole shouts. "They're monsters! Killers! They've committed genocide for god's sake!"

"Genocide?! How have they committed genocide?"

"They tore out parts of other worlds! Even if they rip out only a few acres, what do you think happens to the rest of a world when a chunk of it is literarily torn out of existence? It's done! Everything in that world is dead! Every life. Poof. When a portion of the sky from another world is shared with ours, don't you think that would mess up that world royally?"

I hope beyond hope that Cole is just guessing. Or bluffing. How could he know all this?

Cole walks up to me and points to his face. "What do you think happened when I was plucked out of my world? The two people I'm made from had their bodies sliced apart. They're dead because your heartless parents wanted to save one worthless life! They deserve to know what we're going to do to their beloved daughter."

Cole stomps over to Synister, grabs her hand, and pulls her to the basement steps with him. The Creepers rise and follow them down the stairs.

As afraid as I am of what they're planning to do with me, I can't bear for my parents to witness my fate, whatever it may be. What they've done makes me sick to my stomach but my love for them runs deep.

As I'm staring longingly at the darkened computer screen, the back door opens a crack and Beth sneaks in. She has a finger to her lips as she approaches.

"You're okay," I whisper.

Beth pulls out a pocketknife. Seconds later, I'm free.

"Follow me to the pond," she whispers. "I'll get you back home."

Beth races to the back door and exits, with me tiptoeing after her. Footsteps and voices are coming from the basement. I glance at the computer screen where my parents appeared just minutes ago. Lost, alone, and lacking any hope of freedom. They may have done immoral things, tortured and killed children, and possibly even destroyed entire civilizations. But they are my parents and I don't have it in me to abandon them. Clicking the back door shut and bolting it, I rush to the chair, drape the ropes around my ankles and clasp my hands behind my back, just in time.

Synister and Cole appear at the top of the stairs and a chill ripples through me. Maybe I should have followed Beth to the pond and taken her home with me. My parents would surely want their only two children to be safe. Everything they did was for my survival. Too late now. My choice has been made. The right moment to make my move is coming!

Synister flicks the monitor on. My parents don't seem to have moved.

Cole comes right up to me and sticks his face in mine. It takes all my willpower to not drop the ropes and stand up.

"You're not going to like what's coming," he snickers. Then he sidles over to Synister and puts his hand on her backside. Glancing at me with a mischievous smile, he says, "What next, Babe?"

"Get another chair and set it beside her," Synister orders as she inputs data into the computer. "I'm almost ready."

Cole drags over a wooden chair and places it about two feet away. He picks up the helmets, sets one on the floor in front of me and one in front of the second chair.

Not being tied up anymore has given me more backbone. "What now, tough guy? You going to kiss me again and tell me how wonderful I am?"

Synister spins her head around. "You kissed her?!"

"Babe, it was just part of our plan. You wanted her to trust me." Cole puts his arm around her shoulder.

She shakes it off and glares at him, then punches a couple more things on the keyboard. "Let's do this! Soon I'll be as beautiful as she is and you won't want to kiss anyone else ever again."

Synister sits down in the empty chair and smiles menacingly in my direction. Brimming with smugness, Cole picks up the helmets again, and then frowns. He examines each one closely, likely trying to figure out which one goes on whom.

"What are you going to do? Switch bodies with me?" I get a cramp in one arm from holding them behind me, and almost drop them.

"Not quite." Synister is watching me like a hawk. "I've used your parents' notes, as well as information I've extracted from them to complete the project they were working on."

She nods at Cole. He places a helmet on her head and adjusts the strap under her chin.

"What project were they working on?" I ask nonchalantly, watching Cole saunter over to the computer. The keyboard clatters as he inputs more data.

"They planned to use the healing environment in the Garden to completely cure one of your duplicates," Synister replies as she stares across the room at the computer screen.

I wince and breathe into the cramp in my arm before she returns her ruthless gaze.

"Then, they would bring you here and switch all the genetic elements in the healthy subject's body with your own. Ultimately, when the subject's genetic makeup was transferred to you, the Garden's ability to heal would be permanently ingrained in your genes. You could then go back to your world and live there in perfect health for eternity. You would go from being a very sick girl to being the healthiest person in the universe."

"And now *you* intend to be the healthiest person in the universe?" I ask. "You obviously haven't thought this through. I'm far from cured. As soon as I leave the Garden, my illness will return."

Cole places the other helmet on my head. I don't resist while he roughly adjusts the strap under my chin. They can't find out that my arms and legs are untied until it's exactly the right time.

"Yes, I'll be sick and prone to an early demise. But I'll still feel and look better than I have in years, and will live in a world like the one I was stolen from. And you...you'll bear the torment I've endured for years, suffering for eternity while I live your privileged life."

"Privileged life?!"

"You may have been sick, but I've been tortured like a lab rabbit. After what your parents did to me, my skin burns like it's on fire. My organs feel like they're going to explode. The insufferable pain never ends!"

She didn't deserve to go through what my parents did to her. But I don't deserve it either.

"I will grow up receiving your aunt's love and comfort," Synister taunts. "I'll inherit your family's wealth and estate at eighteen and enjoy life to its fullest until my time comes. *You* will inherit my suffering, while I live the royal life you never appreciated."

"Never appreciated?!" I scream as Cole pulls a wire from the right side of my helmet and searches for the correct socket on Synister's helmet to plug it into.

The Creepers are wandering away, following the scent of the fish, unnoticed by everyone except me. The right time is fast approaching!

"No matter how sad I was about the loss of my parents, or how much time I spent lying in a hospital bed, I've appreciated every second of life." With a quick glance over at my parents, I stand up, the ropes falling to the floor, and savor the shock and horror on Synister's face. "Neither of you will take even a second more away from me!"

I pick up the chair and smash it against Cole's head. He staggers to the floor and crumples into a heap. Synister leaps up and tries to scuttle a safe distance away, or so she thinks. The wires from her helmet drag me with her. I grind my feet to a halt, unstrap my helmet and throw it at her. She ducks in the corner by the stairwell, fumbling with the strap on her helmet.

The two Creepers lunge at me. I dash out of their way, squeeze behind the computer terminals and find the two pieces of fish in the tangled wires. I scoop them up and sprint for the front door with the Creepers chasing me. I open the door wide and toss the fish outside. As soon as the Creepers are safely outside, I slam the door shut, bolt it and turn to Synister.

"Coleus! Stop her!"

Cole is lurching to his feet in a daze. As he staggers toward me, I smash the other chair over his head. It shatters, leaving only a wooden leg in my hand. Cole falls to the ground, stunned.

I march over to Synister, who is cowering in the corner, her helmet at her side. There is fear in her eyes for the first time.

"I have sympathy for what you went through," I say. "I really do. But I did nothing wrong and my life is not yours to destroy."

I raise the chair leg and Synister flinches. But I have no intention of striking her with it. Instead, I stride over to the dome that's glowing blue, bend down and smash the small yellow dome under it. Synister screams as I smash it several more times to make sure the device is destroyed.

Cole is back on his feet and shambling my way, wincing with pain and blinking as blood trickles into his eyes. "You don't know what you just unleashed," he hisses.

I hit him several times in the face with the club. He falls on a table filled with computers, toppling it and all its contents.

"I know exactly what I unleashed," I say and glare at Synister. "Creatures you treated as prisoners when you of all people should have known better."

Synister tries to grab the club but I shove her to the floor, and then swiping the club back and forth like a mad person, smash keyboards, mainframes, and monitors, destroying every monitor except for the one displaying my imprisoned parents.

Cole gets up and we stare at each other from opposite sides of the blue dome. "You useless, filthy bitch," he says with so much despair it hurts.

This conjures even more rage. I lift the chair leg up over my head and smash it down on the blue dome. The glass shatters, exposing a machine on the table, with a purple haze around it.

Synister grabs my shoulder and without thinking, I turn around and wallop her in the chest with the club. She falls backward and Cole lurches forward with his hands out, the evil expression instantly wiped from his face.

Now, he looks fearful. "Stop, Syn. You win," he says with a sincere plea of defeat. He glances from my club to the machine in the purple fog, worried that I'll destroy it. That's exactly what I do.

The first time my club smashes the machine, chunks of metal fly free. The second time, purple sparks flicker. The third time, sparks shoot out. Cole tackles me to the ground as I hear thunder roaring outside. He lets go as heavy rain begins drumming against the roof and tears across the room to Synister. Her eyes are open wide, like she's seen a ghost. She collapses into Cole's arms.

"No!" he yells.

Mucus is building up inside my lungs. I lift my hands to my chest and drop to my knees, coughing. My other is in much worse shape. Synister's face is bubbling furiously as she dangles like a rag doll in Cole's arms.

"Do you know what you've done?!" he screams.

With my symptoms returning in full force, I'm coughing too hard to answer. Synister is withering away. I know exactly what I've done.

Synister looks at me and then at Cole, opens her mouth and tries to speak. She chokes, gathers her strength and tries again. "She's…broken too," Synister whispers to Cole. "Get her home. Let her live."

"No!" Cole pleads.

"Do it for me," my other says, and slumps her head against Cole's shoulder.

And then I watch myself die.

Chapter 35

Dire Consequences

IT WAS NEVER MY INTENTION for this to happen. I killed her. And I'll never forgive myself.

Cole cries silent tears as he holds Synister's limp body. Her soulless eyes are still wide open. The feelings I thought he had for me pale in comparison to the love he obviously had for her.

My symptoms intensify. Cole will come after me soon and do who knows what. I restrain myself from coughing so I will not draw his attention. Forcing myself to stand, I bolt for the back door.

The rain is pounding down. It's cold and my clothes are drenched before making it halfway down the stairway. Even though my hand is gripping the handrail tightly, three steps from the bottom one foot slips and launches me down onto the wet concrete. I land on my hands and cough freely a few times. Surprisingly, there is no sign of the Creepers. Maybe they're hiding from the storm, just like normal dogs might do. Pushing myself up again, staggering from another coughing fit, I follow the path past the cemetery.

It's haunting to think that versions of me—innocent children torn from their worlds—are buried there. Strangely, there is no dizziness this time. It occurs to me that there is nothing left holding their spirits to the Garden. In a way, I'm responsible for their deaths as well. I hope they're at peace now that their souls have finally been released.

It's only been raining for a few minutes and yet pools of water are forming on the concrete path and the grass beside it. In my condition, I shouldn't be out in this weather, or trying to run, but there is no choice. Coughing every few yards, I stop and look behind me to make sure that neither Cole nor Synister's pet Creepers are on my tail. It feels wrong to think of her as Synister now. But what else can I call her?

Frequent flashes of lightning brighten my path every few seconds. I take a wide berth around Cole's cabin, as if expecting him to burst out and tackle me. He was probably rarely there. That's why he had so few possessions. He was usually at the house—with her.

Circling around the pond, I see a beam from a flashlight up ahead. Please let it be Beth. Something trips me, the force flinging me flat on my face. After taking a moment to recover, I stand up to see what tripped me. Not what. Who. It's Wolf. He's not moving. As I put my fingers on his neck to feel for a pulse, a voice interrupts me.

"He's gone." Beth is drenched and holding a flashlight.

She puts her arm around me and momentarily, everything is forgotten; what happened in the house, the horrific things my parents did, Cole and the Creepers, my sickness, the rain. Then a coughing fit seizes me.

After it passes, I gaze into my sister's beautiful brown eyes. "I did this. I killed him. I broke the machine that kept people here from dying."

"It's not your fault," Beth tells me, but I know otherwise. "We need to get you home. The lightway you came through is at the bottom of the pond."

"No, it's gone. I went down and checked."

"There was a stone slab over it."

"Come with me," I plead. "I won't leave without you."

My sister smiles. "Okay."

There is no time to express how happy that makes me feel because a bobbing light from another flashlight is approaching. It's Rose, panting and out of breath. She shines her flashlight on Wolf and runs over to him.

"What happened?" Rose squints at the sky as a flash of lightning illuminates the field, instantly followed by roaring thunder. "What's going on?"

Suddenly, Cole reaches through the shadows and grabs me from behind. "She did this. *She* killed him. Syn killed everyone here."

Rose opens her mouth. No words come out.

"Don't hurt her," Beth demands with such strength and bravery that it's impossible not to admire. "She needs to go home or she'll die."

"I want to snap her neck for what she took from me." He shoves me away. "But my love's last words were to get her home and I won't betray her."

I cough and taste blood. "Beth's coming with me."

Cole grabs Beth by the shoulder. "No. She stays here with me. If you want to free her, you can come back to the Garden and trade your life for hers."

"No!"

"I'll be okay," Beth tells me.

Cole glares at her. "No, my pet, you won't be."

He faces me with an evil grin and hurls me into the pond. The fear in Beth's eyes and the confusion in Rose's follows my backward plunge into the water.

The water envelops me and invades my throat, as I sink to the bottom. Fear of dying and never seeing my sister or Aunt Ruth again is numbing. We were so close to being a family. Now, there is no strength left to fight with. But, as I begin to black out, I see the light and feel a fragment of hope.

Chapter 36

The Vow

THERE IS ONLY BLACKNESS. Then light shines on five faces—Mom, Dad, Beth, Lily, and Flint. They stare at me with expressionless faces. My parents' faces fade into nothingness. The three remaining faces bore through me for what seems like eternity, until Lily and Flint gradually turn to each other. When their eyes look into each other's, their faces contort with terror. They scream at such a high pitch, so piercing, their faces begin to burn. The screaming goes on until their faces are nothing but black ashes, which break apart and float away. Once the ashes have dissipated, they're replaced with Cole's face. Unlike Beth, who is expressionless, Cole wears a sinister grin. His face spins to face Beth and her blank expression turns to fear. Fear and anger. Cole lets out a menacing laugh. The fear on Beth's face fades. Only anger radiates from her now. With piercing eyes riveted on me, she speaks for the first time, not much louder than a whisper. "You did this, Syn. You killed us all."

I wake up, lying on my back. The bright fluorescent lights take a moment to adjust to. I'm attached to an intravenous drip. There's an oxygen tube in my nose. I am stuffed up and congested. Nothing new.

Aunt Ruth is sound asleep, slumped in a chair next to me with her feet stretched in the direction of my bed. I don't think I've ever been so happy to see her. How worried she must have been. She was always here for me. My parents weren't. I had no right to take out my frustrations on the person who willingly replaced them. The one person who has always supported and loved me. I never showed my aunt the love I've always had for her. That's going to change. Starting now.

I allow her to sleep. As eager as I am to show her I'm okay, there is a lot to think about. My parents have done horrible, unspeakable things. That said, they are my parents and it pains me to know they are trapped in that soul-sucking, empty bubble. And even worse, at Cole's mercy. I think about dear Beth. My sister. What Cole might do to her. What I have done to that beautiful Garden. Wolf is dead because of me and who knows who else. That's all on me.

"Syn."

My aunt is awake. She rises, wipes away my tears and gives me a gentle hug. She's crying too. "Thank god you're okay."

She holds me for a long time. A nurse comes in and then the doctor. They check me out and tell me I'm recovering well and might need to spend a week or two in the hospital to receive treatments.

As the nurse adjusts my IV, a man in a suit walks in and shakes my aunt's hand. He introduces himself to me as Detective Carroll and she leads him to my bedside.

"Are you well enough to speak with the detective?" Aunt Ruth asks.

"Yes."

He explains that another officer pulled me from the pond. I tell him that I don't remember anything. Just that I was sitting by the pond and then woke up in this hospital bed. It's a complete lie but what else am I supposed to say, especially with my aunt listening? That I went to an alternate reality, which my supposedly dead parents created? Where they were trapped by another version of myself?

When the detective leaves, I tell my aunt that I love her. "I'm going to say that more often."

After another hug, she kisses my forehead and tells me to get some rest. I am tired but need to ask her one thing, even though I'm pretty sure what the answer will be.

"Janna...?" The very answer I feared is on my aunt's face.

"I'm sorry," she says. "Janna passed away the day after you visited. Her funeral was yesterday. I really am sorry."

The world feels different, knowing that Janna is no longer in it. Empty, like it no longer makes any sense. She was beautiful inside and out. I cry myself to sleep.

When my eyes flutter open again, the world still feels hollow. I look to my left and instead of my aunt, Ebby and Jon are sitting there watching me.

Their eyes are puffy from crying. Ebby immediately stands up when she sees I'm awake. I put my hand out for her to hold.

"We were so worried," Ebby says. "I'm so glad you're okay."

I have no doubt that she's been worried sick. Maybe it was because Janna and I were so close, like sisters, that I couldn't admit any other friendships were real. Maybe I wanted to feel sorry for myself because she was dying. But Ebby cares. Holding my hand comforts her. And I have to admit, holding hers comforts me.

Jon takes off his glasses, wipes his eyes, and swallows nervously.

"Hi Jon," I say, trying to make it easier for him.

"I'm sorry," he says. "I did a horrible—"

I stop him right there. Compared to the things I've done, he's a saint. "It's okay. I understand."

"You do?"

"Yeah. I don't really want a boyfriend right now anyway. But you do know what I could use?"

"What?" Jon asks through sniffles.

"Another really good friend. If that's—"

Jon doesn't wait for me to finish. He lunges for me and wraps his arms around my shoulders. "Yes, friends." He cries some more.

Ebby rolls her eyes and sticks her finger into her mouth like she's trying to barf. I smile at her, but keep my laughter inside so I don't hurt Jon's feelings.

The world may seem empty with Janna gone but accepting other people who care for me as my friends will help over time.

I sleep for most of the day. Doctors and nurses do tests while I'm awake. My aunt escorts me for short walks down the hallway. At the end of the day, a nurse gives me pills, I use inhalers, have a few treatments, and then the lights are dimmed. My aunt sits next to me and falls asleep before I do.

Though feeling very tired, I lie in bed for some time before even considering sleep. There are fond thoughts about Janna and another good, long cry. I think about Beth, but knowing I have a sister comforts me for less than the second it takes to recall the image of her in Cole's grasp.

Facing Cole in the Garden will be even more dangerous now that there are no elements to curb my CF symptoms or protect me from injury. But I have no intention of leaving her there with him.

The thought of Beth being trapped by Cole for even one day is sickening. However, it wouldn't be smart to return before recovering, or without a plan. I don't intend to just show up and turn myself over to Cole. My life is much too valuable to just give it up. Nevertheless, I will come up with a good plan while I recover. And when I am healthier, I vow to return to the Garden and save my sister from that two-faced monster. Maybe even free my parents, if they are still alive.

I've always valued each and every day of my life as a gift and couldn't imagine having it cut short even by one single day. As the image of Cole threatening the life of the sister I never knew replays in my mind, realization strikes. I know the odds of rescuing Beth are not in my favor, and yet something has changed. Despite my yearning to live for as long as possible, for the first time in my sixteen years, my view on life is different. Along with my renewed thirst for life, a picture of my sister's face is firmly planted in my head. This image makes me realize something I had never considered before—that some things in life might truly be worth dying for.

EVERYONE DIES
IN
THE GARDEN OF SYN

Book Two in the Garden of Syn Trilogy

Coming Soon

Join Michael Seidelman's mailing list at www.michaelseidelman.com to be notified of its release.

Acknowledgments

First and foremost, I thank my parents, Shelley and Perry Seidelman, for all the support they offered me while writing this book. They were the first ones who read my manuscript and provided me with a ton of valuable feedback— both positive and negative—that helped me build a stronger story for the next group of readers. I thank Tracey Lutz, Lorne Greene, Lillea Brionn, and especially my sister, Sara Solomon, for their constructive critiques. Thank you to Dr. Mark Gelfer for verifying the medical information. Any mistakes are my own. Thanks very much to my editors, Davina Haisell and Geoff Smith, and to my talented cover artist, Kimberly at KimG-Design.com.

My extensive research on cystic fibrosis included watching countless YouTube videos of teenagers detailing their challenges with the disease and sharing their struggles and daily routines. I wish I had kept a log of these videos so I could thank them personally. Their openness and honesty helped me understand the realities of living with cystic fibrosis more than anything I had read on the topic. The video diaries are heartbreaking and inspirational. I hope that a cure for CF is found soon so that all the wonderful kids and adults living with the disease can enjoy the long and healthy lives they deserve.

And a big thank you to everyone who read this book, reviewed it, shared it or recommended it to a friend. Writing fiction is my dream job and having this book enjoyed by as many people as possible helps make all my dreams come true!

About the Author

When Michael Seidelman was growing up, his passions were reading, watching movies, enjoying nature and creative writing. Not much has changed since then.

Working in Online Marketing for over ten years, Michael felt it was time to pursue his passion as a career and wrote the first book in The Garden of Syn trilogy.

He is currently writing the second and third books in the Garden of Syn series and, beyond the trilogy, has many ideas plotted out that he looks forward to sharing with the world!

Michael was born in Vancouver, BC Canada where he continues to reside.

You can learn more about Michael Seidelman and join his mailing list at www.michaelseidelman.com. You can also follow him on Facebook, Twitter and GoodReads.

This story is fiction but cystic fibrosis is very real.

70,000 children, teenagers and adults in the world suffer from the disease. While treatment is far above what it once was, there is still no cure. Let's help find one.

Please check out these sites for more information on cystic fibrosis and how to donate to help find a cure.

Cystic Fibrosis Foundation (US) - https://www.cff.org

Cystic Fibrosis (Canada) - http://www.cysticfibrosis.ca

Cystic Fibrosis Trust (UK) - http://www.cysticfibrosis.org.uk

34032607R00171

Made in the USA
San Bernardino, CA
16 May 2016